CW00540659

THE WELLS OF UR

The Wells of Ur

Norberto Argentavis
JB Jackson
Jon Mollison
Brian Renninger

PILUM

Nantes

2022

THIS IS A BENT MISSILE BOOK,
PUBLISHED BY PILUM PRESS.

Cover design and typesetting by Luisa Editorial. Copyediting
and proofing by Chicago Inferior. Power-to-weight ratio and
deadly aim by John Carter and the Riddle of Steel.

Illustrations:
Schuyler Hernstrom (p20);
courtesy of Basham & Winstead (p54);
and Penny Melgarejo (p76).

ISBN: 978-1-956453-01-0

Published March 2022

When a man rides a long time through wild regions he feels the desire for a city. Finally he comes to Isidora, a city where the buildings have spiral staircases encrusted with spiral seashells, where perfect telescopes and violins are made, where the foreigner hesitating between two women always encounters a third, where cockfights degenerate into bloody brawls among the bettors. He was thinking of all these things when he desired a city. Isidora, therefore, is the city of his dreams: with one difference. The dreamed-of city contained him as a young man; he arrives at Isidora in his old age. In the square there is the wall where the old men sit and watch the young go by; he is seated in a row with them. Desires are already memories.

—*Italo Calvino*, Invisible Cities

CONTENTS

ALL CITIES ARE DEAD CITIES

An introduction

What was the movie, I often ask myself, a child of the seventies who grew up in the eighties and became a soldier in the nineties, that changed me from a child to a survivor? A watcher of late night sci-fi movies and reader of books about the day after tomorrow when Morlocks rule and handsome young men of science try to rally the Eloi into taking some responsibility. What was the movie where atomic-blasted dead cities lay gray and sketched on the horizon, and all the stories contained within them, the shattered windows, the forgotten doll with one eye, the yellowing newspaper with the doomsday date that declares some dire "Russkies Drop Big One" which intrigued me so? Must have

9

been some kind of *Planet of the Apes*, end of civilization, we finally blew it all up post-apocalyptic cinematic thriller melancholia that did it to me as a kid and made me who I'd be a constant observer, and professional liar, or writer, if you prefer. And ever since, I've been fascinated by dead cities. Go figure that most of my stories revolve around them.

All cities are dead.

Even the living ones where people are moving around, running off to work, catching an Uber, sitting in a café and reading the paper, trying to be hip, cool, informed, and not make eye contact with the human wreck in the corner nursing that all day coffee the baristas do their acts of charity by, pressing their hand in the mud of eternity and hoping there's some kind of simple salvation in kindness for the sake of kindness.

Maybe the wreck is a writer. Probably. But as I said, all cities are dead. All cities have been around long enough, even the ones out here at the edge of the known world, California, or maybe the end of the world to come, all cities have dead people who once caught that trolley, penned a jingle they were going to run by Frank in advertising while they ate a ham salad sandwich and drank a cup of black coffee on a thirty-minute lunch. There's a double header out at the park that day. And of course avoiding that human wreck in the corner who was just some poor American down on his luck. Maybe a writer—probably so, even back then.

But those people are all gone now, and only their city stories of jingles, or ham salad sandwiches you couldn't find now if tried to in the age of Avocado Toast Empires—even that double header in which the kid caught that uncatchable ball deep in left, and the grand hero who was in his last season before the cancer got him, came out just long enough to wave at the crowd. Those stories, those people, they're all gone now.

The human wreck and the paper reader staying up on the scores, or the opera, are all gone now. The factory is now a market collective, the warehouse a hipster loft. Some pizza places remain the same. Thankfully. Every building, every grave, every yellowing piece of paper is a story of a dead city that, if you look close enough like I do often, staring up a the gray and dirty cracked homunculi on an old building face, or caressing the red brick inside the hot new gastropub that used to be an ironworks, wondering who set that brick. Where did they eat their lunch, what was the opera of their lives as they worked at laying that wall, long ago, in a dead city, not this one anymore. Who were their heroes, and those must have been amazing deeds...

All cities are dead, and someday... Some day, even now, this city, will be dead, too.

Fascinating. There are so many stories inside a city.

Look on my works and despair.
Some human wreck who went by
Ozymandias. Probably a writer.

*—Nick Cole, West of Moon, East of the Sun,
February 2022*

MANHATTAN TO BUENOS AIRES ON THE BETSY ROSS

Foreword

I came in underground. I forget the last thing I saw before it all went dim. I began in Annapolis—or Baltimore, I guess—on the Betsy Ross. Anyway, I embarked in sea air and tall trees that walked beside us for miles. Then trees crunched down to coastal scrub. The color dropped out as we drew near. Memory supplies industrial brownfields but I had turned away from the window. A naval cadet on leave read the *Sun*. Nobody had a laptop, tablet, or a mobile phone. I carried an *en face* edition of Lorca's *Poeta en Nueva York* because that is the guide you carry in your jacket pocket when you want to better pile mystery onto the chaos you're about to enter.

A certain pressure pervaded the air in the compartment well in advance of arrival. The cadet rolled his paper into a tube and tapped it on his knee. Although everyone was still seated, there was a building press to leave. When the time came, I wheeled my way through the crowd at Port Authority and was recovered by my sister. We went off , a level down, arm in arm, beneath the earth.

Back then, people came together by remembering the number of the train, the hour of arrival. Trains, like the Betsy Ross, had names that were common knowledge. Not just brothers and sisters—we were all present to each other, were capable of meeting at appointed times and places. We didn't slovenly vector each other around the city by buzzing messages back and forth. No. We asked directions from other people. Bodega owners said which streets to avoid. Restaurant advice came from taxi drivers. All was spoken out in broken American.

My sister and I ended up at the wrong stop. There was fury in the evening air. Meaning and incidence became densely allied. One had to translate the city, read in another language. Everywhere, there was a subtext of aggressive humor and industry. Everything was piled on everything. A shove in the subway was information. A couple of leaning toughs breaking away from their basketball pack was a warning. Fortunately, a kindly-spoken, overweight cop ambled over and guided us back to safety. That night I listened to pistol fire.

The towers still stood.

So, here they are, two fictions which re-count the bang from which urbanity begins. And two fictions recording the whimpers with which it ends. All four seem as reliable a guide for any traveler resolved to the possibility of embarking at Camden Station, Baltimore, only to emerge at Salguero Street, or Café Groppi, or before the Synagogue at Budapest. Limits of time and space are nothing to these worthies.

"Granary records," say the Sumerian language experts, "So many tons of barley in late summer."

"A list of excuses for missing work days," says the Ancient Egyptian language expert, "This dude claims a scorpion stung his foot."

Both experts deliver lives from beyond the dust barrier. They read stone and bone, the ul-timate dual-language edition. If history were a bone, Jon Mollison's "The City at Dawn" would take us into history's marrow, or within whatev-er is deeper than marrow. He takes us beyond mute runes—a task too important to be left to mere language experts. Only audacious imagi-nations like Mollison's can render the moment when a city became socially possible. His fiction speaks louder than ruin.

❀

I've never, not even once, visited Philadelphia by car without having my vehicle rifled for its frost scraper, floor mats, stereo system, and chewing gum. Long before this became common practice in San Francisco, I learned to leave my doors open, and to cross my fingers that nobody would defecate in my Fox, or Polo, or Focus. But that was then and the 1977 of JB Jackson's "Philadelphia" is even grittier—if not the slough of despond, then just upstream. The narrator's good humor and wit, while locally hilarious, are grim counterpoint to a general degeneracy.

Brian Renninger's "Across the White River" begins with a playful high drama, a chaos of weird churn which asks "How do we know when greatness is born?" How do we know when we have been given a gift? What do we do about the arrival of a stranger with a vision of order so strong it takes root by itself? Finally, how can we build *anything* if we aren't willing to come to our city's defense?

"Do you have time to stop by again?" I had just spent an excellent, sunny afternoon at the Buenos Aires apartment of the writer Alejandro Manara. I was walking past the polo grounds, contemplating joining the crowds on the lawn at Plaza Mitre. I was enjoying the freedom of being in a remote city. "I just opened the mail," said Alejandro, "You'll want to see this." I gave up on my nap and turned around.

My Spanish is really only okay. Even with Alejandro's help, the sun had gone down by the time I puzzled my way through a rough translation of the first paragraph of *Elektra and the Laws* (Elektra y el orden). Such was my first encounter with Norberto Argentavis.

"Who the hell is this guy?" I asked.

"He's really interesting," said Alé, "Teaches geography and history. Likes that weird fiction you like."

"I don't know," I said, already exhausted.

"You'll be in Rosario tomorrow," said my old friend, "Meet for lunch. See if you get on."

For me Rosario, Argentina's third city, is a garden sand spit under a magnolia tree where I once played plastic soldiers with my second-cousin Eduardo. My great-grandfather made his residence there, in apartments which now house a fine arts school of classical dance. Argentavis, on learning this, insisted on taking a *collectivo* across town to Sarmiento Street. The building, an *hotel particulier*, would not be out of place in the Sixteenth in Paris. I don't know whether this founding Durando had it built to his design, selected it out of a book, or whether it already stood when he paid off the notary. "This neighborhood was slapped up in less than a decade," Norberto said, gesturing at the elegant facades.

Every city is patterned on an ur-city, an agglomeration of echoes. I think I can tease out

Chicago, Milan, Córdoba, Barcelona, Paris, Rome, Budapest—even the towered farragoes of Jodorowsky, Moebius, and Hergé seem to loom over Argentavis's work. Its splendor is only partially conveyed in my inadequate translation.

I suffer a terrible disorientation when I emerge from the subway in Sheridan Square in Manhattan. I can no longer discern up- from downtown. The towers, at once absent and re-placed—but once reliably *south*—used to true my needle to north. At least everyone, at the time they were destroyed, agreed upon whom to blame. This time around? Blame for the current state of our cities has already been laid. The inevitable scapegoats might even turn out to be the guilty parties. But surely the coming penalty will cobble together as tight and final as a tomb.

Excuses for this sorry state of affairs are slowly filtering up between the pavers, like grains of the famous, yet illusory, beach promised by Parisian rhetoric in 1968. *Beneath the cobbles lies a beach*. Nobody ever cared about sunbathing—the slogan was a poetic way of duping dumb kids into prying up the paving stones so they could later be hurled at the police. I've seen the so-called rejuvenation cycle at least twice in my lifetime. I'm really not sure my father's Buenos Aires is better than the one I last found in 2016. I'm certain that the city where I live, is very much worse for the wear since last season. Engines for stern reform are being stoked. Imagination informed by enthusiasm, nostalgia, and regret will be their fuel. A real builder's vision withstands any force. Even crowds. While we're waiting for the confrontation, why not slide this paperback into your jacket? Let it ride over your heart. It might well protect you from the knives glittering in the shadows.

—Neal Durando, Nantes, January 2022

THE WELLS OF UR

Unknown,
translation by Norberto Argentavis

When our city was
Undermined by the sea
The last spirits were decanted,
Into clocks indifferent
to the liquors by which the hours were
kept.

It was worse once the sea withdrew from
the quays
We watched the moon consume itself
Brewing tea laden with lower salts
We knew would wind us to a sooner stop.

We brewed tea laden with the lower salts.
Barges became camels became peddlers
addled by wide horizons.

Our ships stood on their keels.
Our dead became denatured.
Our hollow wells howled to the stars.
The evening wind rose
To meet an absent tide.
Breezes haunt the sheepfolds.
The campfires of a nomad horde
Discrete beyond the rubbled walls
Fearful of our vaulted ruin.
Our thoroughfares bathe under the light
Of hostile constellations.

We once drank from beneath the sea,
From beneath the storied earth beyond,
From wells not sunk from above,
Pushed up from the higher world.

—Fragment, fin dynastie Ibbi-Sin, ~VIe siècle av.

THE CITY AT DAWN

Jon Mollison

Translated from glyphs scribed upon a tablet of baked clay, recovered from the wreckage of a Roman-era cargo ship. Discovered on the floor of the eastern Mediterranean and believed sunk by an early winter storm, AD 190.

O man! We children of Enki, who came into the world as babes. How short our memories, how frail our respect for our forefathers' stories, how easily lost are the annals of our genesis!

Only the infinite prudence of the gods could have guided the tortured steps of your humble servant and led him to the ruins of that pre-Pharaonic vault of antiquity. Years of quiet study led to moments of terror out in the trackless sands of the western desert. Disease took the caravan first, then bandits picked over the bones, until only poor Namurur remained to stagger, unthinking upon that lost repository of the ancients, that vast tomb to lost knowledge upon which scribes millenia ago related their own discoveries.

The reading of those runes took time, even with my years of experience. Clean and simple were the carvings, and a pleasure to pore over, to ponder, and to decipher. A sense of connection with the scribes responsible for the walls of writing arose. This unnamed scribe lived as far in time from the subjects of his tale as your humble servant lived from this unnamed scribe. We both sought evidence of the first days of mankind. This scribe had not merely pieced together that tale, he labored to record it in unchanging stone. To record it for all time. Our lives were separated by vast chasms of time, and yet were we not of one mind? Were we not of one heart? One liver? Could any man in that position not feel a kindred affection for his forebear? I ran my fingers across the time-worn inscriptions and wondered. I wondered, will a man read these same words, five millennia hence? And upon reading, might he not feel such a kindred for your humble servant?

The thought terrifies and invigorates.

Primitive by our standards, the tale follows no modern path of a simply stated, true and profound chronicle. Unadorned with the vital testimonial embellishments modern educated men cherish, the tale may echo strangely in the ears of mighty Samsu-Ilina. Pray, do not judge that ancient scribe upon harsh scales. Instead, O mighty Samsu-Ilina, place all fault at the feet of your humble servant, whose meager talents can scarce bridge the chasm of two languages and five millennia that lies between us. All praise be upon the brow of mighty and just Samsu-Ilina, without whose prudence this tale would be lost. All thanks be upon the hands of that nameless scribe. All blame be upon poor Namurur, who serves as dogsbody between the great man of today and the wise man of yesteryear.

Young eyes see only near horizons. In his youth, mankind saw only the dangers of the shadows and the giants who drove his fathers from green and pleasant valleys. Fearful, man wandered in blood-tied bands, eked out a meager sustenance. Always did he live in flight from other clans of men, and in terror of the raids of the Big Men and Shadowmen, who of old would pluck the young and the pretty from the clans of the First Men and carry them off to their cooking pots. The terrors lived in the verdant land between the deep and broad valley of the Big Men and the dark and mysterious leaf-shaded halls of the Shadowmen.

Until there arose a champion among men who lifted his brothers out of misery of discord.

The Champion, fair of mien and broad of shoulder, led the Tribe of Lions and suffered no defeat in battle. With the death of the enemy chief assured in every duel, and the spines of his lesser warriors so often stiffened, the Lions rampaged among all the wandering tribes. They challenged all whose paths they crossed. First for women and plunder, and then for strength of honor and pride of victory. Their larders fat and their families bursting with children, even the Shadowmen learned to cower within their jungle bowers when the Lions neared.

For long years, they grew in wealth and strength. The Champion grew restless. His people had won against every other tribe. The Tribe of Ravens scattered rather than fight. The decimated Tribe of the Jackals followed in their wake, challenging tribes depleted of their best warriors. The Tribe of the Elephants fought nobly, but fell beneath their hardened spears. Likewise the seaside Tribe of the Dolphin, the forest dwelling Tribe of the Wolf, and the desert dwelling Tribe of the Scarab. The Tribe of Bears put up a titanic struggle, and the great duel fought amongst the men lasted for three days and three nights before the last of the Bears succumbed and gave honorable defeat. All fell before the Lions, save one.

The Tribe of the Eagle lurked on the edges of the lands of the First Men. Swift of foot and light of purse, they eschewed strength of arms and material need, preferring instead the safety of mobility and an honest gratitude for a life free of the restrictions of goods and treasures. They had a reputation for cowardice, even as their women gained a reputation as great prizes both for their fair looks and great health as well as the rarity with which they were encountered in the camps of other men. Few were the tribes that could corner the Eagle and force him to battle. Fewer still were those who could corner the Eagles with wind enough left over in their lungs to offer valiant battle.

The Champion knew well of the Eagles and much desired to make a trophy of their spears and their women. All of the tribes now melted away at the approach of the strengthened Lions. The Champion grew weary of the tedium of rule which his people forced upon him. He chafed at the minor quarrels of his over-large tribe of lesser warriors. He lived for combat.

Though strong in body, he also possessed a cunning mind. He knew that capturing the Eagle would require more than might of arms. He gathered his chief advisors, the wifeless and nattering men of his tribe, and bade them offer a solution to the puzzle of the fleet-footed Eagles. After a full season of council, he threw up his hands in disgust and kicked dust in the faces of the holy men.

The Champion called forth his warriors, from the greatest to the least. He commanded them to pack only their spears, their shields, and food enough to carry them through a ten-day journey. Against the wishes of his wise men, he commanded all others to await the warriors' return.

"O great Champion," the elders wailed. "Think not of glory! Think of thine people! The AllFather will surely curse you for abandoning us here! Alone and defenseless with our enemies all 'round? Surely shall we perish!"

But the Champion guessed that the learned, elderly men only desired after their own safety. He spat in the dust at their delicate feet. The lethargic life of council and rule would not be his. He desired only the heady rush of battle and the intoxicating thrill of glory. He much preferred the feel of a spear in his hand to a tribe at his feet. And so he set out with his men to trap the Eagles and bind them to his wrist.

On the horizon, the Eagle tribe's outrunners observed the dust stirred up by the horde of Lions. They guessed at the reason for the great stampede of men, and raced back to their campfires where the leader who commanded their path, the First Eagle, guided the tribe away from this approaching doom.

Lacking the speed to catch the swift-legged men of the Eagle, the Champion sent forth his best runners to shadow them. If the speed of the Lions would do them no good, perhaps their great numbers might. He flung small bands of men out toward his flanks. The runners were to make the distance between his forces too narrow for their prey to pass. In this manner he shepherded the Eagles south and south again for nine days. On the tenth day, when his men grew weary and their stores ran low, did the Eagles finally reach the green wall of the hot jungles, beneath whose towering boughs and behind whose green ferns did the many watchful eyes of the Shadows gleam with deadly malice. Caught, the Tribe of the Eagle turned and faced the Lion.

There, on the plain, at the edge of the jungle home of the Shadows did the two tribes meet.

Now the leader of the Eagle Tribe earned his place not by might of arms, but by swiftness of body and mind. Slender as a reed, and stolid of visage, as were all of his people, the First Eagle was no less honorable than the towering and powerfully built Champion. Recognizing that the countless Lions had clipped his people's wings, the First Eagle at last strode forth to meet the Champion in battle.

His woman appealed to him to forgo the rites of combat.

"Take the better part of your warriors," she cried. "Melt away into the jungles and depart to live on and continue the Eternal Wheeling about the Earth." Well had she noted the hungry look in the eyes of the Champion when he gazed upon her long flanks and lovely countenance. So too had she noted the clean lines and power constrained within his limbs, and she knew—as all that day knew—that the fight could end only with the death of her man. Perhaps her heart sought to save the life of her man. Or perhaps the gold that lay in chains upon the breast of the Great Champion pulled upon baser emotions buried within her. Or perhaps, victim of the weakness of the flesh of her kind, a longing for safety within the great Champion's iron thews played upon her. Her position as First Woman of the Eagles lay in doubt, and in those long passed days, sorely did any man or woman relinquish power.

Who can say at this long remove?

Whatever lay within her heart, her man would not be swayed.

"No, my love," he professed. "For you are young and lovely, and even for a chance of your safety and freedom to fly, gladly would I die." In his heart he guessed that the brutish and slow Lions would tie her free spirit to the earth and she would never again feel the wind of her passage blow through the long locks of her hair. "Nor would I leave even the least of my brothers behind to face the ravages of the Lions in my absence. Though the end be not in doubt, truly must I face the Lion alone."

He left her then, his heart heavy, and she with a tentative hand lifted to her fearful frown.

With great reluctance did the First Eagle respond to the ritual challenge of the Lions and accept the call of battle. For in his heart, he knew such a battle could end in naught but the death of his tribe, and in his wisdom the

First Eagle proved aright. Though perhaps for much the wrong reasons.

The two chiefs met in the open land between lines of warriors, and made and accepted the traditional challenges.

And then did a strange thing happen.

A shout rang out from afar. The fastest of the wise men of the Lion had arrived with perilous news.

The frail men's words had come to pass.

The Big Men watched the fires' glow along the heights grow faint and, from that sign, their blockish thoughts supposed the dwarves on heights distracted. They crept up the walls of their valley and so fell upon the defenseless women and children and the frail men of the Lions. While the Champion pursued his own glory, and threw his men southwards in pursuit of the Eagle, the people of the Lion came to ruin. So great was his sorrow that he almost shattered the long tradition.

The Champion bade his Lions to pursue, to quit the field and turn to chase the Big Men, but the warriors of the Lion stayed his impetuous hand. "Great Champion," they cried. "The bonds have been sealed. The oaths have been sworn. Would you betray your word, and so profane our precious traditions?"

But the Champion would not be swayed. "And will your precious traditions warm your bed anights? Sharpen your spears betwixt battles? Birth thy lineage that they may carry your

31

name down through the ages? Nay, I tell you now, not even the spoils of victory shall comfort you for the loss of all else you hold dear."

But his men would not be swayed. "You," they implored, "you who have never lost in combat, and who have led us so nobly for so long–shall you now command that we quit this field in supplication and shame?" And likewise did others mutter, "Whatsoever thou might save among our people will surely be forfeit unto the Eagles–yes, and unto all other tribes." For truly and rightly did they judge that all the tribes of men would exult in their humiliation at the hands of the Eagles.

Seeing thus that his men balked, the Champion relented of his desire and set about ordering his men with great swiftness. Never was the circle of combat, ten paces across, scratched upon the ground and marked with a ring of low stones, laid out so swiftly. The Champion arrayed his men with no hesitation, in the traditional order of greatest to least with himself the first to enter the circle.

But the First Eagle desisted. He hemmed, and he rubbed his chin in silent ponderings. Long did he labor over which of his men to send into the ring of stones. With a cunning and ruthless callousness, he goaded the Lions into nervous skittishness.

Among the stunted trees that ringed the place of battle, the Shadowmen whispered and goaded the men of both tribes to greater heights of bloodlust. They sensed a rich banquet of misery and pain this day, and flitted about in exuberant celebration.

"Come now, Eagle Man," the Lions cried. "The day is old and the conclusion foregone. Cease your womanly fretting and have done with it."

The First Eagle lifted a hand to quiet their impatient shouts. "It is a fell thing to enter battle unprepared," he said. "And the ancient rites proscribe no limits to my contemplations." With a gesture, he ordered a fire to be built, and his long pipe and tobacco brought forth. Settling down to feign a deep deliberation, he allowed the men of the Lion to whip themselves into a great fervor of impatience and anticipation.

Only when the First Eagle judged their patience upon the point of breaking, did he speak the name of his chosen first.

Of old, the two tribes paired the best warriors in the circle first, and then the next best, and so on through to the weakest warrior. Here now, the First Eagle nominated one of his youngest warriors to face the Champion! To the surprise of none, the young warrior died nobly and bravely within moments of the Champion's first charge. Thus insulted, agitated, and confused, the Lions that fought in turn strove with an impulsive haste to prove themselves the better warriors. For those with the eye to see, a pattern soon emerged in the fights that followed.

Each Eagle who entered the ring eschewed the savage attacks practiced by most men. They preferred a lithe and defensive approach to battle. They waited for their foe to tire, to wear himself out in his unthinking fury, and when such transpired, they leaped forward, putting their speed and stamina to good use.

The Lions who entered the ring stood tall and proud and fought with the unthinking savagery of their namesake. Many did not tire at all, but beat upon the Eagle's shield with unrelenting strength that drove their foe to the sand.

In such manner the Eagles who earned glory did so through speed and cunning. The Lions who earned glory did so through strength and fury. And when neither man survived to leave the circle under his own power, the duel was declared honorable and by the ancient traditions chalked as an impasse.

With studied precision, the First Eagle had matched his warriors carefully against the Lions. He pitted his worst warriors against the best of the Lions, sacrificed them in defeat to ensure victory by the greater number. In such manner, the quick and cunning Eagles had fought the larger and more ferocious Lions to a standstill. When the final two combatants entered the ring, each of the tribes had won an equal share of glory.

The Eagle who entered the ring for the final test proved to be the First Eagle himself. The last of his warriors, the fate of the day rested in the strength of his spear arm. He had sought to secure victory, the greatest of his warriors against the least of the Lions, and been foiled by the cunning of the Champion. For the Champion, though proud and stubborn, was not stupid and the moment he judged the First Eagle's plot, he withheld the best of his warriors for this final round of decision. Thus did the First Eagle face not the greatest Lion nor their least, but only one typical of the breed.

The Lions and the Eagles who survived the battle now crowded close around the ring to witness one final throw for victory and glory. Lion mingled with Eagle, elbow to elbow around the great circle, as the two warriors orbited each other. Great was the battle that pitted the strength of the larger Lion against the speed of the Eagle. A savage blow from the Lion found no purchase in the flesh of the elusive First Eagle. Blood wept from a dozen cuts along the flanks of the Lion, yet he fought on. Their wicker shields torn to shreds, they fought with naught but spear and fist. With every wound, the Lion's anger grew and his desperation rose until at last he abandoned all thought of self-preservation and threw himself upon the spear of the First Eagle. The copper blade stabbed clean through his flesh and wedged itself deep into the bone of his shoulder. The Lion threw an arm around its haft to lock it in place whilst his spear hand drove low. Weary and unable to avoid the blow, the First Eagle twisted away only to feel the blade sever the tendon of his ankle.

The watching Lions and Eagles drew back in shock. Each recognized a wound that, while not fatal, left a warrior defenseless against his foe. The First Eagle scrambled away, dazed by the dullness of his speed. A lifetime of quickness on his feet vanished with the flick of one spear tip. He struggled to adjust to the limp given him by his foe. Unable to maintain his grip on its shaft, he released his spear, whose blade remained within the flesh of the Lion and whose butt settled into the dust of the ring, a third leg which held the dying Lion upright.

The Lion breathed heavy and wet. He struggled to lift his own spear, blood flooding down his chest and side to carry his vitality down, down, down to soak the earth. Determined to honor his tribe, he flung his spear with a leaden hand, and so great was his fortitude, and so helpless his foe, that the blade struck home. Not a powerful killing blow, but strong enough to smash into the First Eagle's leg and drive him down, face first, into the dust where he lay motionless, pinned to the earth by the spear through his knee.

All round the circle, the world grew quiet. The warriors of Lion and Eagle shifted uneasily. No animals disturbed the silence. Even the Shadows who watched from the trees ceased their hoots and howls.

The warrior Lion died with a smile on his face. Having slain his killer, the duel between tribes had concluded in a draw. His comrades, the strong who had survived, could honorably turn away now to pursue their women into the lands of the Big Men.

So thought the Lions and their champion, who sought to disengage from the place of the duel until a weak groan from the First Eagle stayed their retreat.

"The duel is not yet ended," sighed the First Eagle.

They looked on in amazement, and an Eagle made to tend to his leader's wounds.

The strong hand of the Champion stayed the man's approach.

"The duel is not yet ended," the champion echoed.

A bare three strides separated the First Eagle from the circle drawn in the dirt. With one ankle ruined, one knee shattered, and his strength spent, there could be no doubt of the outcome. The man for whom running was a way of life could not hope to drag his body across so great an expanse, and yet he flung out a hand to grip the Lion's spear holding him motionless. With a great cry, he heaved the spear free of the grasping earth. He flung one hand out, the soil gave way beneath his hands, and he grunted with the exertion, but with a heave, he managed to cover a bit of ground.

The warriors of the two tribes quieted, oblivious to the whispers in the trees around them, and waited for the completion of a race between the First Eagle's strength and the distance over which he had to fight. His body advanced in fits and halts and stops. The spear that felled him served the First Eagle well, as he thrust it down into the earth, now making of it a handle upon which he might pull to gather a few more handfuls of distance and push behind him.

Twin trails of red marked his passage as he fought. The First Eagle's head crossed the circle, then his chest, but his strength was insufficient. Once, his eyes rolled back and his head fell forward, but the voice of the Champion called woke him with a shout. "Come on, man! Get up!"

For the Champion may have been proud and stubborn, but he recognized a kindred spirit when he saw one. He would fane have jeered or insulted the brave figure writhing his way through the dirt. All true men stood ensorcelled by the grinding crawl of the First Eagle toward victory for his tribe, some in hope and some in dread, but all in fascinated respect.

And the Shadows quailed and fretted. They howled and jeered at the First Eagle and bade him surrender to the sweet surcease of toil. "Sleep well, brave warrior," they cried in their discordant language. "You have fought well. Now rest." For their weak minds sensed a change in the winds. An understanding among the First Men that threatened them in ways they could not name.

And still the First Eagle crawled, across one slim handful of earth at a time.

Thus did the First Men fall prey to the dishonorable perfidy of the Shadows, who chose that moment to creep from the line of trees. With the low cunning of their kind they slipped toward the men around the circle, bearing bone-tipped spears and stone-tipped clubs. It was the shout of the Champion, the exhortation of valor thrown toward his foe, that caused the First Eagle to lift his eyes for but a moment. And there in the gathering gloom of the setting sun did the First Eagle spy, beyond the Champion, a spreading line of black limbs and glowering menace.

Galvanized by fear, the First Eagle rolled to one side and flung the Lion's spear, black with the mud of his blood mixed with earth. The barb flew out beyond the Champion, who fell back in surprise at the seeming betrayal. His surprise transformed to rage at the sound of bone-tipped spear on flesh and the grunt of a Shadowman as his progress toward the Champion's unprotected back was checked.

The battle that followed proved short and the defeat of the men of the Shadows inevitable. Lacking the numbers and strength of arms of the two combined tribes of First Men, they retreated back into their dark bowers, carrying their dead with them.

And thus it was amid the clash and roar of battle that the First Eagle threw out his last reserve and edged his unfeeling feet over the line of the circle. And thus did the Champion find him and cradle his weary body and lift a skin full of cool water to his cracked and dry lips.

"O great leader of men," the Champion cried out. "You who have given me life, and you die, so shall I. But if you live, then so shall I repay your gift of life with mine own loyalty until the course of my own life joins the sea of the afterlife."

His men gasped at his words. They had lost the duel, but that meant the loss only of plunder and women—things they could recover from other tribes within a few seasons. Only when the vanquished tribe had withered to too few in number to survive the wild did a leader throw the last of his lot in with their conquerors. They still numbered twice the Eagles and with the better part of the better Eagle warriors slain, they could return to deal vengeance at a later time. For the Champion to declare the stricken First Eagle as his King was unthinkable.

For his part, the First Eagle thrust away the waterskin and replied, "Nay, for have you not also saved my own life from the perfidious ways of the men of Shadow? Could I protect even myself from them with mine legs shattered so? Nay, I say again. Yours is the better part of strength and valor, and should I live, I would pledge fealty to you. For is it not known that a leader must protect all his people, and could I even protect myself like this?" He gestured at his ruined legs—so swift and proud they once were—and could not imagine that even the weakest of men would ever again show him the least honor.

"A leader must also be wise and cunning," the Champion replied. "He must love his people above all else, and in all three ways have I failed. You led my men upon a merry chase. I would live to see the chase you might unleash upon the Big Men."

"Your time grows short to save your people," the First Eagle countered. "My convalescence will end only with my own death. Leave me and do your duty to your people. You need swiftness now, and I have none."

"My people are your people. Make of me your right-hand, the blade with which you stab at the world. Do this for me, and I will serve you with all my strength."

But the First Eagle did guess that the Champion's motivations were not selfless. "Admit one thing to me, and I shall grant your wish." He spoke now not just to the Champion, but to all the men around them. For he guessed rightly that the men around them had already begun to plot and scheme and jockey for position and rank in the newly constituted tribe whose quickening was heralded by their conversation. "You have the spirit of a warrior, and you would escape the contrived plots of the council hall. You would escape the nattering demands of the elders and the wise. You would seek comfort and peace upon the field of battle, would you not?"

"Aye," said the champion. He lowered his head. "Not for me the tangled webs of politics."

"And can you live content to honor my wishes, though they cut against your instincts?"

"I can."

"And so you speak before all those assembled here?"

"I do."

"And will you grant me first choice of women among the Lions to take as a wife, that my children will be cousins to your own?"

"I will."

"Then let it be as you command, O great champion and hero of mankind. Let me live out my days showing your honor by fulfilling this, your final, command. From this day forth, let our tribes be joined!" So spake the First Eagle, and when his pronouncement elicited no enthusiasm among the men, he recognized their doubts. What matter his own lineage when theirs hung in a balance so delicate? He spoke on to quell their worry. "But not as Eagle or Lion, rather as Eagle and Lion joined together as one. As a child is comprised of both mother and father, let our new tribe be joined a child of lion and eagle." With one blood drenched finger, he drew a figure in the sand, with the body and strength of a lion and the wings, beak, and talons of an eagle.

And so did the legend of that mythic creature we now name Griffon enter into the world.

The men, sensing a beast with the heart of both proud animals, strong and swift and fearless, now hailed the First Griffon as their leader. In time, the historians of those long dead people came to know the First of the Griffons as the Cripple King, and so shall we name him in these annals.

In his first years of reign, the Cripple King ruled a fractious people. Never before had so large a tribe existed, and they saw not how it might be managed. In those first days, however, they were subdued and much plagued by doubt. The enthusiasm for the birth of this strange new world was dimmed by the plight of their newfound king, and the need to hasten to battle with the Big Men.

For one night only did they linger there upon the border with the men of the Shadow while the First Griffon convalesced. On the morrow, they set out at a pace languid by the standards of the former Eagles. The Cripple King rode in the arms of the Champion, and they made plans as they marched north to the great valley. The lesser part of their warriors they left behind to protect the women and children who yesterday bore the sign of the Eagle, with orders to follow as best they could. The greater part marched north to battle, and here the swiftness of the former Eagles proved as valuable as the strength of the Lions.

Runners and scouts raced forward to the rolling green hills of the wide valley, then hastened back to report their findings. In this manner, the Cripple King could pick and choose his time and place of battle. Men had known of such methods, their keen eyes always wary of such ambushes as they passed through high grass or deep fen or shadowed wood. The baser animals that skulked in shadows swiftly dealt death to unwary men. From time immemorial had men disdained the use of such trickery in battle. Dishonorable and cowardly they were, but the Cripple King judged that his warriors would meet their doom without them.

While struggling to find words that might convince mighty Lion and swift Eagle of the need to adopt the ways of their namesakes, the Cripple King noted the green shoots of a new weed in the minds of his men. For during the journey between the place of the duel and the land of the Big Men, the warriors of the newborn Griffon fell into old habits. Eagle lay 'round fire with Eagle. Lion lay 'round fire with Lion. Only a few daring warriors dared to sleep around the same hearth with a recent enemy. When they marched, they marched in two distinct knots of men rather than as one band.

The Cripple King watched these sad tidings with keen eye, and soon devised a plan to break the old bonds and forge new ones among them. If no longer would men fight alone in a dusty ring, they must find a way to fight as one body made of many souls.

They made camp upon the cliffs of the great valley, and every night looked down upon the cook fires of the Big Men. Every night they wondered which of their women or children might be stewing within those cauldrons. Readied were they to march into battle, but also much afeared, for the smallest of the Big Men stood a full head taller than even the Champion The elders and the wise muttered that the Big Men had been birthed by demons and that the strength of their arms was the least of their powers.

In their mind's eye they saw one after another duelling ring drowned in the blood of great warriors, all squashed into jelly beneath the clubs and stones and fists of the Big Men. How could true men hope to prevail against such giants?

The Cripple King was to show them.

Seated on a rock at the very edge of the cliff side, with his back contemptuously set toward the land of the Big Men, he assembled the warriors who would stride into battle. They stood arrayed before him with blunt-tipped spears ready to practice for the coming fight. The Cripple King bid the Champion to step forward into the field of grass before him. The Champion did so. Then he commanded three warriors to stand ready.

"But which of us, O King, should stand ready first?" they asked.

"All of you," he decreed. "At once."

They stiffened in shocked confusion.

"But my King," the Champion said slowly. "This is not the way of war. We have no circle."

"And did the Big Men draw circles upon the earth the night they stole our women?"

A light of understanding entered the eyes of the Champion. "They are not men. They do not honor the old traditions."

The Cripple King nodded, and judged the time right to lay bare his plans. "We must learn a new way of fighting. As the Lion joined Eagle, so too must warrior join warrior. As our tribes are greater now that they fight as one, so too must our warriors become greater by fighting as one. My Champion, I am skilled in the ways of the spear, but mine shattered legs cannot dream of how to work with those of others. Tell us, how might these three warriors act as one?"

In such manner, with the Champion working the puzzle from within and the Cripple King observing from without, they did devise a new manner of fighting. Shoulder to shoulder in a line, with spears thrusting forward and shield protecting the man at his side, they found themselves forced to trust their counterpart. Their old allegiances would mean nothing when the Big Men came bellowing forward. And so they trained for three days upon the clifftops, and the Big Men jeered their defiance at the strange dancing of the First Men. They laughed as the First Men paused to discuss and plan and strategize, mistaking their cunning planning for cowardly weariness.

The laughter ceased when the First Men surprised them early the next morning.

Even before the sun appeared above the horizon, the First Men clambered down the long steep slopes of the great valley. Carrying only shield, spear, and light provisions, they rushed forward through the dawn to spring upon the nearest camp of the Big Men.

The Big Men were born of the tears of Ra, and had about them the same appearance as the First Men save for their size, their long and apish arms, and a simian countenance that made them terrible to look upon. They had lived from the first amid the lush garden-like pleasantness of the wide and deep valley, which produced numerous soft fruits unbidden. Nuts and berries fair sprang from the ground into the waiting hands of all who hungered, and the Big Men had lived easy lives bereft of the challenges that drive men to force their will upon the earth. Only the capture of fat and lumbering hogs at first, and in their later rapacious lust for the women of the First Men, did the Big Men find reason to think beyond the next few moments of life. And even in these tasks did they find their great strength more than enough to compensate for the slow and dull and brutish thoughts that churned beneath their thick craniums.

So it was that they did not take even the most rudimentary of cautions when laying abed. And so it was that they died, still snorting and snuffling atop the piles of skins they used as beds, when the First Men crept down into the valley in pursuit of their captured women. Great was the slaughter that first night's skulking raid effected, and in the days that followed the Big Men threw themselves at this band of interlopers with a wild abandon. In all their previous encounters with the tribesmen of the plains to the south of their home the Big Men ran rampant. Unable to understand how the dwarfish men managed to drive so deep into their lands so quickly, the Big Men threw themselves at the five hundred strong with ever greater ferocity.

As they flung themselves upon the spears of the First Men, the Big Men fell like wheat before a scythe. Disciplined and determined, the army of the Griffon traveled as one great beast. A hedgehog of deadly points where every man stood his place in line and every spear thrust in the same direction, the Big Men had no counter. When the spirits of lesser men failed, the champion always stood proud, a blessed figure ready to stiffen their spines and remind them of their place as first among all Ra's children.

Soon the Big Men learned to fear the First Men, who swept the lands long after cutting loose their stolen women. Their blood up and quietly determined to avenge a thousand years of privation, they harried the dwindling numbers of Big Men from one end of the valley to the other. With every forward step, the green and pleasant land was claimed by those brave and stalwart First Men.

The Big Men clambered out of the valley and disappeared into the tiny ice-strewn isles of the northern seas or disappeared into the vast green halls of the western forests that blanket mountain and plain. Their numbers have dwindled ever since, and to this day some few small tribes still lurk in deep caves or on forlorn, rocky isles. Glimpses of them can be seen by the wary and the wise, and women still spin tales of the Big Men to frighten small children into behaving, lest they disappear into the cook pots of these hulking and stupid and now secretive beasts.

Long was the celebration there among the lovely abundance of the garden that covered the valley. Gladly did the Champion's betrothed honor his command and give of herself to the Cripple King, who treated her gently and raised her up.

Bitterly did the First Eagle's betrothed accept the hand of the Champion on behalf of her people, and in her jealousy did she sow the seeds of discord among the tribe of the Griffon. For her desire to escape from the Lions rose not from fear of their predations, but fear for the loss of her standing as First Woman of her tribe. To be thus reduced from queen to princess was a slight that left her sore aggrieved, and long did she hector the Champion and make for him a displeasing home. And yet, even in her petulance did Ra work great things, for as her ire waxed wroth against the Champion and make of his home a place of unrest, the Champion ventured forth ever more often to release his frustration upon the enemies of the Cripple King, and to slake his thirsts among the women of the tribes conquered by his arms.

And conquer he did. With the Big Men gone, the Champion of the Griffons swept aside all opposition to the Cripple King's ambition. The people of the Ram fell. The people of the Scorpion fell. The people of the Jackal and the Cobra and the Tortoise all resisted and were laid low. And their women fell to the charms of the Champion, and did distract him from any lingering thoughts of rebellion against his crippled friend and brother.

And so were all the men assembled under the banner of the Griffon for the reign of a hundred kings. To honor him they built a palace on the high plains, a place of great beauty and gentle slopes that he might hobble along in peace and serenity, dispensing wisdom and guidance from within a grand hall as majestic as any firelit vale. For how could the Cripple King accompany his armies on the march with his legs bent and broken? How could he defend even himself? They encased their leader in a safe prison of stone and luxury, and as they built this first palace their own homes sprawled outward along stone paved lanes. And men came to sow and reap grains in all the fields all around.

Even before the last stone was laid in the palace's foundation, the agglomeration of man swelled to the largest assemblage in man's young history.

The elders and the wise saw a chance at improving their own lot, and encouraged all men to contribute to the endeavor. Beneath the Cripple King's sheltering shadow, those who heard the voice of the AllFather assumed places of great import. They partook themselves of leisure and beauty and soft beds and fine feasts. While the strongest and mightiest of the Griffons marched forth against their enemies, to sleep upon hard ground and eat of cold and modest repasts. In this manner rose the triune balance of man, a great king and strong armies and learned elders, that can be found in every civilization since.

Though the name of that long lost city has been lost to time, her primordial influence echoes down through the ages, and in them we find much of ourselves.

Thus ends the annals of those nameless scholar-priests who wrote in strange glyphs and signs upon the walls of a mighty store of knowledge. The last glyph showed a rising city amid long sweeps of grain fields, carried aloft on the backs of hordes of slaves and servants. It shows mankind united as one under the guidance of a Crippled King, and mankind's united desire to erect a tower so mighty as to pierce the belly of Heaven itself. In our legends, we recall the fate of that project, and by its example do we hope to succeed where they failed.

Here now at last is my labor ended. Here now at last, after a long recuperation in the warm embrace of the fortress-palace of Babylon, have these words been recorded. May this history never again be lost to mankind, and in such manner may it glorify the name of great and wise Samsu-Ilina, and not, despite my countless labors, the name of the poor and unworthy chronicler Namurur.

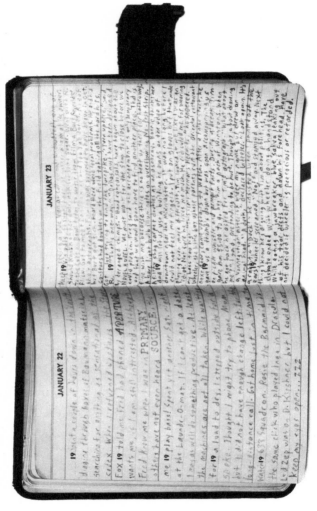

Basham & Winstead (San Francisco).
De re dordica: Items from the Seaberg Collection.
December 8, 1997. Sale no. 818.

PHILADELPHIA

an excerpt from Shagduk, *a novel*
by JB Jackson

TUESDAY, APRIL 19

Expressed concern to Dr. Lanier about going to Philadelphia, who replied in W.C. Fields's voice, "I'd like to see Paris before I die. Philadelphia will do!" He said I could just go to a clinic there for my shots and scribbled an address on a slip of paper. Probably could have used this as an excuse to skip the conference, but I was stoked about seeing Danh again on Porteous's dime.

Picked up my new glasses on the way to work. The frames are similar to my last ones, but not quite as good, of course. Nothing ever is these days. Buy American!

No response to my interlibrary loan request for the Henry Bell book. Too rare to loan, I guess.

Encountered Randy in the break room. "Dude, what were you thinking?" he said.

"Huh?"

"That poster you made. Dordic?"

"I couldn't help it," I chuckled. "So you're the one who took it. You bastard!"

Randy looked hurt, but then said, angrily, "You're going to blow our cover."

Our cover? An interesting choice of words. But he has a point.

WEDNESDAY, APRIL 20.
Tashi is performing at TCU this evening. Had they been playing the Messiaen, I would have been pissed to miss it.

Picked up Diane in the Rambler so we could catch the red-eye to the City of Brotherly Love. What did the City of Brotherly Love do to earn that handle? Having heard stories about lost luggage, I figured I could just take my mansack and a duffel bag. On my weekend book hunting road trips to Austin, Houston, and San Antonio I usually just take a toothbrush. Diane, on the other hand, brought her entire Samsonite collection, which looks like the ape got the best of it, and several clothing bags.

"Is that all you're bringing?" she said. "Do you have a jacket?"

"I'd only end up lugging it around."

"Where are your shirts?"

I patted my duffel bag. "Wash-and-wear."

As soon as we got settled on the plane, Diane whipped out a tattered Mary Stewart omnibus. She had not been talkative in the car, either, but perhaps she is not an early bird like me. Passed the time drawing sunglasses, blacking out teeth, and adding beards to everyone in the in-flight magazine before cracking open *Rogue of Siluria*. Diane's skirt was hiked up, exposing a lot of thigh. It always seems like it is on purpose with her. Unlike Jenny's mixed signals, I can tell Diane is not into me. It is more like she wants something from me. But what? Recalling my recent conquest of Jenny, I wondered what a spell on Diane would accomplish. If I called her bluff, how far would she go? All the way? I can see why Randy is cautious.

Takeoff was uneventful, but I found myself gripping my novel nervously. Diane never looked up from her own book, so I assumed she was an experienced flyer. Was prepared to admit I had never flown before, but she did not ask. Once the stewardess brought her a Bloody Mary, she loosened up a bit.

"Oh, Miss," she said. "Would you bring me a pack of cigarettes?" Diane turned to face me. "Did you see her outfit? Halston."

I nodded in agreement. "This plane seems really nice. Almost opulent. Feel like I should have worn a tie or something. Damn it, I forgot to bring a tie!"

"I have a scarf you can wear," she said, wryly.

"Is it Halston?" I lisped. What a bitch. Was privately relieved that I did not have to wear a jacket or tie now. Unless Diane narced on me to Dixie. But what would she gain from that?

"Ugh, an infant," said Diane, crossly. Across the aisle, a squirming baby make sounds of discomfort. His mother gave him a binky, which seemed to do the trick. Such easy, natural magic. Meanwhile, the passenger behind me tried to force his knee through the seat and into my liver, lodging it there for the duration of the flight.

After what seemed like an eternity watching baggage on a conveyor belt, we waited an hour for a taxi. Five people begged us for spare change, including a couple of Hare Krishnas. To each his own, but I am not shaving my head for love or country. Already did that once.

The cabbie flipped a uey that sent my head knocking against the window. "We're not in a hurry, driver," I barked. This was my first time in a taxi. "Is it always this hard to hail a cab?" I said.

"Fucking transit strike," muttered the driver.

Diane was flirty with the cabbie, which I found irritating. Was it necessary to touch his arm like that? What did she stand to gain?

At the Commonwealth Club there was a mix-up with our rooms. They had a reservation for Diane but not for me. There were no other vacancies.

"But I specifically asked for two rooms," argued Diane, loudly and somewhat melodramatically. Before I could suggest that the concierge find me a room elsewhere, Diane said, "Why don't we share? We're just going to sleep there. We'll be out doing things."

Was just about to concede when the manager appeared and had a quiet conversation with the desk clerk. "We have a room in the basement," said the manager. "It's rather austere but clean. You may stay in it free of charge."

"That is kind of you," I said. Turned to look at Diane and I swear I saw her shoot the manager a dirty look.

Diane's room shared a lone bathroom down the hall. Imagined long lines in the morning just to brush one's teeth, but then found out there were only six rooms on two floors. Not sure why Diane chose this place to stay. Classy. Felt like one had to be a member to stay here, but Diane probably would not be. Pretty sure she is from California. Know little about her, really. Or California, for that matter. Where did she work before Porteous?

My room was as described, but had its own bathroom. After depositing our belongings in our respective rooms, Diane and I took another taxi to the Bellevue-Stratford, where the conference was being held. The driver played tour guide, pointing out various points of interest in a stream-of-conscious monologue. His cab looked like he lived in it. Next to him on the seat was a cardboard box stocked with beef jerky and tins of sardines and Vienna sausages.

"Behind these handsome walls you got your Eastern State Pen. Al Capone was a guest of honor. Big Joe Bruno. Over there you got your Museum of Art. You seen *Rocky*. You like presidential plates? They got your American Presidential China exhibition. Caught us at a good time, weather-wise. Freezing sleet in your face, then a week ago we were in the nineties. Ever try wooter ice? Ah, nothing beats Fluffya in the spring."

Philadelphia must have been ground zero for bicentennial madness. Everywhere I looked there were images of Uncle Sam, thirteen-star Betsy Ross flags, and the Liberty Bell. Ben Franklin's smirking mug. Tableaux of Ye First Thanksgiving. Red, white, and blue detritus in the gutter. A man in a tricorn hat shouted at us as we passed. Something about Redcoats and big discounts.

"Over there you got your library. Checked out my first book there in '52. *The Codfish Musket*. Ever read *The Codfish Musket*? That's your Logan Fountain. Toss your coins in that beauty. Make a wish. What do you wish for?" After pausing for a reply, he continued. "A cheesesteak from Mickey's, that's what you wish for. There's your City Hall. Next stop, the Bellevue-Stratford. Careful don't catch Philly fever in there. Had a bad outbreak last year."

After paying, the driver turned around and looked at us. When he saw my long hair, he said, "You gonna see the Dead at the Spectrum on Friday? I'll be there. Saw them in '73. Terrific show. Was up front at the rail, thanks to my buddy Cheeser who got us in early. There were a bunch of guitar strings from Bob and Jerry on the stage in front of us so they could change strings. See? I still wear mine around my neck."

Diane and I just grinned at each other. Deadheads are nuts.

"Alright, then, youse have a good stay now."

After the mayhem of registration, Diane and I quibbled over what to do first. "The NBTCG Budget Assembly starts soon," she suggested.

"Let's go in here," I replied, pointing into a crowded exhibit hall. A bikini-clad model wearing granny glasses and stilettos was chained to a brand-new bookmobile on a slowly revolving platform, shushing anyone who ogled her. Diane and I wandered down the aisles, listening to pitches and taking in the scene. We collected pamphlets and free samples in canvas tote bags with "Gerstenslager" or "F.W. Faxon" on them. One booth featured a pedestal with a granite ball floating in a fountain. The ball was seemingly weightless though it probably weighed about twenty pounds. When I reached for it, some suit yelled "Don't touch!" As Diane and I moved along, we could still hear the guy yelling at other people not to touch the ball. By the time we reached the other side of the exhibit hall, our tote bags were full of notepads, pens, rulers, and other freebies. Scored a "Librarians Do It Better" mug. Diane's prize was a ball-point pen shaped like a syringe and filled with red ink. She brandished it playfully.

"Bend over," she said.

"Where did you get that pen?"

"From a guy in the Medical Institute Press booth. He also gave me his number, like I would ever call him from Texas."

"I'm sure he did," I muttered.

The rest of the morning was coffee and cigarettes until I told Diane I had to run an errand. Her face fell. Felt guilty for ditching her.

"I'll be back in time for the 'Information Please' panel," I said.

The address to the clinic was illegible. I realized no one would know if I blew off my injections. Even if I were sick, rabies shots were not going to help. Instead, I lingered in a record store before racing back to the conference. Took me a while to find the North Hall, by which time the panel was concluding. When I took my seat next to Diane, she looked at me and scowled.

"Sorry I'm late. I forgot which time zone I was in. The banquet starts at six-thirty. That gives us just enough time to have a few drinks beforehand. Saw a bar I want to check out. They must be open by now."

On the way, we got a couple of wooter ices. We ducked into an antiquarian bookstore. I paused to study a Turkish dictionary. When I caught up to Diane, she was reading a book.

"When a man," read Diane, "Under some pretext or other, goes alongside a woman and touches her body with his own, it is the touching embrace." I leaned away from Diane so our arms were no longer touching.

"Let me see that," I said. I examined the title page. "The *Kama Sutra*. Jim Croce's copy—what do you know?" It was only three dollars, so I bought it.

Should have known a place called Bookbinders would be packed full of A.C.L.A. refugees. We ended up sharing a table with a group of librarians from Milwaukee. Handed out a few of my custom matchbooks which were well received. Everyone was drinking heavily.

The banquet was a disappointing affair in a huge hall with too many seats and not enough people. Diane and I sat alone at a table for ten.

Offered Diane some of my spinach soufflé. "It's people!" I cried, impersonating Charlton Heston. Diane busted a gut laughing, but it was not that funny. Someone was making a speech at the other end of the hall, punctuated by scattered applause. After nearly picking clean a crustacean tree, I moved on to the Hawaiian frankfurter platter and salmon avocado mold, the latter compromised by an excess of mayonnaise and olives. The great thing about buffets is that you get to try a little of everything. By the time I got to the Bananas Foster the champagne (and booze from earlier) had caught up with me. Diane ended up

63

helping me to my room after a surreal and embarrassing ride in a taxi I would rather forget. She was kind to me and patiently explained what was happening when I experienced an asparagus urination scare.

While wallering in bed, I felt thirstier than I had ever felt before. Hydrophobia! Skipping my injection was probably a bad idea. But Vietnam did not get me. And neither will Harvey.

Thursday, April 21.
Too hungover to get out of bed. When I answered Diane's knock, I exaggerated my condition, suggesting partial paralysis while raising a limp arm in the air.

"Philly fever," she said, with sarcastic certainty.

As soon as she departed, I showered and dressed. The towels here are excellent. Suppose they will not miss one of them. Walked along busy streets to the Museum of Art where I spent more time in the gift shop than in the exhibits. They offer merchandise you do not see in ordinary stores. Ended up buying a replica of one of Duchamp's *boîtes-en-valise*, filled with miniatures of his most famous works. A shrunken typewriter cover, a tiny glass ampoule of Paris air (which I was tempted to break open and inhale), postcard-sized reproductions of a mustachioed Mona Lisa with her hot ass, etc. Duchamp's female fig leaf predates the Plaster Casters by nearly two decades. Felt like a traveling salesman walking around with it. "Madame, can I interest you in a pocket-sized urinal signed "R. Mutt"?"

After quitting the museum, I paused to watch a group of Japanese tourists posing like Rocky on the front steps, fists raised in triumph, shouting "Adrian!" My trek down Ben Franklin Parkway took me past the fountain the cab driver had showed us. Sculpted frogs and turtles spouted water at a group of river gods by Alexander Calder. Saw no resemblance between these and the Bank One Eagle back home. A different Calder? I fished a nickel out of my pocket and closed my eyes. I wished for Harvey to go away. If this works, I will believe anything.

Arranged for Danh to pick me up at the Commonwealth Club, where I ditched my *boîte-en-valise* and changed into corduroys. Danh showed up in his '74 Dodge Monaco and honked. When I got in and shut the door, he laid rubber down half a block while I gripped the dash.

Danh's parents live in a suburban brick house surrounded by classical statuary. *The Capitoline Venus, David,* and *The Thinker* flanked a wide, pebbled driveway.

"The discus tosser's missing an arm," I said.

"Myron's *Discobolus*. One of the neighborhood kids was hanging off it when it broke."

Danh's father greeted us in the den. He offered me a cup of tea, which I accepted out of politeness. After some small talk during which he learned I was a musician, he reverently presented to me *The Great American Songbook*. Felt it was prudent to bow, so I did. He then gestured to a Kimball Swinger 700 organ. Barely concealing my panic, I looked at Danh who nodded.

Sat down and turned the instrument on, then experimentally pressed a key. Selected the Leslie effect for a nice vibrato, then opened the songbook and searched for any song I might already know. I pressed another key. Something was not right.

"Because I tried to replace the Leslie speaker fuse twice, and both times they blew out, it is my assumption that the Leslie amplifier is out of order, and I cannot fix it," explained Danh's father in halting English.

The occasion called for a slow foxtrot. "This is 'Beautiful Dreamer,'" I announced. As soon as I started playing, singing falsetto, Danh's mother appeared by her husband's side. The rhythm was slower than I had intended, which dragged the song beyond the four-minute mark. When I finished and turned around, Danh's mother had tears in her eyes.

I stood and took a bow. If I ever got fired from the library, I could do this for a living.

"Nobody notices wrong notes," whispered Danh.

"You stay!" his mother begged and took my hand as we prepared to leave.

"Thank you for the tea," I said. Danh hustled me out the door.

Danh turned onto the Baltimore Pike then floored it through a yellow light. "Open the glove box," he said.

"Brass Monkey?" I said. I took a blast before handing him the bottle.

"I haven't forgotten!"

Danh took the scenic route back to the city. We reminisced about our Primary Source days. Told him about the library, Jenny, and Time Frame.

"Do you still play?" I asked.

Danh shook his head sadly. "Working stiff now. By the time I get home in the evening, I lack the will to live. How do you do it?"

"It's the only way to get the music out of my head."

"Well, it was wonderful to see you again. Send Dixie my love."

Returned to my room to discover the contents of my duffel geometrically arrayed on the bed. The *boîte-en-valise* lay open on my pillow. The ampoule of Paris air was shattered. I sniffed the room, half-expecting to smell the Seine. Instead, I smelled Harvey.

Caught up with Diane downstairs in the dining room. "How are you feeling?" she said.

I sighed dramatically for effect. "Still weak. This Crab Louis ought to perk me up." If Harvey visited Diane, she made no sign.

We ate in silence. Out of the corner of my eye I caught Diane stealing glances at me. As soon as I finished eating, I excused myself. Diane started to say something but hesitated.

"What is it?" I asked.

"There's nothing to do in my room," said Diane. "Was hoping we could go for a drink or something. There's a bar a few blocks from here."

"Let me get my jacket."

The same librarians from Milwaukee were at the bar, partying at the tops of their lungs. The place was a madhouse. I winced as one of them danced upon a one-legged round table to Frankie Valli.

"Are you sure about this place?" I asked. Diane pretended not to hear. The only free table was covered in empty glasses. Utilizing a trick from the codex, we were soon seated at a clean table. Diane stared at me searchingly.

"I could really go for a slow screw," she whispered. Her breath was hot in my ear.

Our eyes met for a moment.

"It's the offspring of a Sloe Gin Fizz and a Screwdriver," she explained.

Am always so uncomfortable ordering drinks at a bar. Can never get the bartender's attention, and they always ask me questions I do not know the answers to. Could barely even hear him over the din. "Surprise me," I replied.

Mine was a Harvey Wallbanger. Surprise, indeed. Felt like Vee was looking out for me. Both drinks were garnished with leftover red, white, and blue umbrellas.

The librarian on the table ate shit as I made my way back to Diane. Assumed she was okay when I heard cheering and applause. Diane was fussing with a fingernail. "I chipped my polish," she lamented. After setting our drinks down, I noticed I had clipped my own thumbnail too short this morning. Damn it!

"What a meat market. Haven't seen such debauchery since Randy and I went backstage after the Emerson, Lake & Palmer show at Dallas Memorial in '74."

When one of the librarians put his hand on my shoulder to brace himself and puked, I rose to leave. Enough is enough. We gulped down our drinks and shoved our way through the writhing bodies toward the exit.

Diane pointed at a neon "Psychic" sign across the street. The door was unlocked. The interior was lit by candlelight. Music binged and bonged from speakers concealed behind spider plants. Incense filled the air. A petite old woman in a white silk robe emerged through a beaded curtain. She wore pale lipstick and eyeshadow. Her white wig was balanced slightly off-kilter. "I am Sylvia," she announced.

"Is this Steven Halpern playing?" I said.

Sylvia just looked at me. We settled on a high price. Sylvia explained that the cards help interpret one's subconscious. "Who's first?"

"My name is Diane."

"What kind of guidance do you seek, Diane?"

"Will I regain what is rightfully mine?"

Diane cut the cards. Sylvia arranged seven of them in a V.

"The first card, which represents past influences, is the Three of Cups reversed. It reveals that what might seem to be an impudent undertaking was a sensible step."

"I'm relieved," said Diane. *Does she believe this stuff?*

"The Seven of Swords. Present circumstances. A dispute involving a friend concerning your personal possessions."

"Yes," said Diane.

The rest of the cards indicated "intrigue and deception" and "delays and disappointments in plans."

"You should accept change if it comes and not act impetuously without wisdom," said Sylvia, rotely.

"I see a profitable partnership. Few obstacles stand in your way. The Queen of Cups reversed tells us that a quarrelsome woman will be thwarted in her attempts to provoke discord."

Dixie! Who else could the quarrelsome woman be? Unless it is Jo Ann. I recalled what Jo Ann had said about Diane.

Sylvia looked at me. "Your turn."

"This is *yaje*," I mumbled. "Can I bum a cig?" I added, patting my pockets.

Sylvia's face darkened. "Knowledge is power," she said while digging in her purse.

"I already know what's going on here," I said, petulantly.

On our way to the next bar, Diane was thoughtful. "Did the cards tell you what you wanted to hear?" I said.

"Yes, I think so."

Diane and I were both pretty shitfaced when we got back to the Commonwealth Club. I ushered her upstairs. When we reached the bathroom in the hall Diane reached for the doorknob. "Oh, no. There's somebody in there," she giggled. "Can I use your bathroom, Steven? I don't think I can wait. Please?"

When we entered my room, I turned on a lamp. "Ah! Bright!" protested Diane, shielding her eyes.

"What are you, a vampire?" I teased.

After Diane came out of the bathroom she dug around in her purse and produced a joint.

I smiled. It was my turn to pee. Thought I might vomit. Stood hunched over the sink for some time. When I finally emerged, I opened the door and nearly tripped over Diane's Famolares. A scarf was draped over the lampshade. Diane was lying on her back and had nearly slid off the edge of the bed. Her skirt had ridden up. I stood there for a moment, wondering how to proceed. The gentlemanly thing, perhaps, would be to let Diane sleep in my bed while I took the armchair. As I reached under her knees to move her, I caught a glimpse of a birthmark peeking out from the edge of her black lace panties. The birthmark was shaped like a butterfly. It all came together. Are Diane and Ursula of Ulm the same person?

FRIDAY, APRIL 22.

A sleepless night in a stiff chair, the strap of my mansack wrapped safely around my wrist, staring hard at what I suppose is an unquestionably dangerous woman. Diane was probably watching me, too, through nearly closed eyelids. What is her game? I showered and dressed before Diane stirred, then waited for her in the dining hall.

Diane and I had little to say over coffee and croissants. Because she had not registered for the Technical Services Roundtable this afforded me some time to clear my head while she wandered the exhibit hall and waited for me. As soon as I knew Randy would be at the library, I got change for a five dollar bill for the long-distance call.

When Hazel answered, I disguised my voice and asked to speak to Randy Kelso.

"May I ask who is calling?"

I said "Mr. Mantee" because Randy would know it was me.

"This is Randy."

"Hey, man, you know that chick Ursula in Austin who drugged me? Guess what? She's Diane."

"What do you mean?"

"I'll explain tomorrow. But what the hell, Randy? Am I in danger?"

72

"Hazel is standing right here," whispered Randy. "Ursula is who you said?"

"Yes. I'm sure of it," I said. "What do I do?"

"You have the upper hand if this individual doesn't know that you know."

"Understood. Here she comes now, bye." I turned to Diane.

"There you are. Come have a smoke with me." Was determined to play it cool. During "Media Centers in Academic Libraries: A Survey" we were almost asked to leave because we were laughing too hard making *cadavre exquis* drawings of the speakers and attendees. My performance was refined and convincing. Do not think she knows that I know what a treacherous bitch she is.

On the way to the airport I tried not to call attention to my *boîte-en-valise*, which I figured Diane would ask about. Caught her looking at it a couple of times, but she did not say anything. Found this strange, but Diane is a strange woman.

The flight home was eventful for two incidents. The first was a passenger who became hysterical over something she saw out the window. Harvey, no doubt, jacking off on the wing. Hope he froze to death but something tells me he did not. The second was when we were waiting to disembark. Diane picked up my mansack to hand to me and predictably spilled its contents all over the floor. This game I knew. Picked everything up casually, but Diane got to *Successful Muskrat Farming* first.

The codex had fallen open to an especially provocative page, bearing a potent sigil.

I snatched the book from her. Rather than offer a lame explanation, I held my tongue for once. Let the bitch wonder. On the way out, I asked a stewardess about the hysterical woman.

The stewardess smiled. "Just a nervous flyer. Thank you for flying Braniff!"

SATURDAY, APRIL 23

Back on Tejas soil. Three days since my last injection. Nurse Irene was a no-show but I am clearly out of the woods. Jenny had lots of questions about A.C.L.A. She told me about yesterday's Earth Day celebrations. She was still celebrating today by wearing her Earth Shoes and her "Give Earth a Chance" button. She was also wearing the amulet, now attached to her black ribbon choker in place of the bell. I sighed.

"Don't those make you feel like you're walking uphill?" I said.

"They make my calves strong. Here, feel."

"Wow. See what you mean." I turned to greet Guddu. "Did you go to the Earth Day party yesterday?"

"No, Steven. Guddu has taken sick leave the last few days."

Noticed my chipped beige desk is a lovely shade of green underneath. Looks like the Rambler. Spent hours peeling the beige layer off. It is much more work than I realized.

Professor Ziglar came up to the information desk. "I'm looking for *The Virtue of Selfishness* by Ayn Rand."

"Here you go."

When he saw Rand's photo on the dust jacket, he said, "A woman? Never mind. I have never read a book by a member of that species, and I never will."

Noticed my "Books To Be Dealt With" shelf is suddenly overflowing. If Guddu was out sick the last few days, when did this happen? Maybe Spunt put them there.

Gig at a party on Luther Lake in someone's backyard. Parking was a pain in the ass, so I had to dolly all my junk down Rowan Drive. The paving was rough. Thought my speaker wires were going to shake loose. We have hit the big time now.

Luther Lake was paradise when I was a kid. There were only a handful of houses around it. Reeds and moss grew all around the edges of the limpid, spring-fed waters. It was full of largemouth bass, channel cat, perch. There were seasonal migrations of thousands of waterfowl of every description. Year after year Canadian geese, mallards, herons, and red-winged black birds roosted there. Used to see beaver, too. The ravine beyond the dam is now a dumping ground. Coasted across in the Rambler so as not to scare whatever wildlife might remain.

"Luther Lake! Are you ready to rock?" cried Tim as the neighbors all peered out through their curtains at once.

ACROSS THE WHITE RIVER

Brian Renninger

It was only through two unexpected events that this story of blood and doom came to pass. Two events that, while small as compared to the heavens, led me to madness. Just as a falling tree can bring down all around it while raising its roots to the sky, so too my madness ended in men falling in droves and the City of Im rising to greater, undreamed-of heights.

Three events, really. But we will get to the third in due time.

The first event was that I, Langadi the Lame, as the oldest warrior had been given the honor (in spite of my infirmity) to lead the bearers of Queen Rabhana's palanquin to the Hiekka's—the desert people's—lands. The

Desert King, Orkan, had summoned her to inspect the queen's quickening. He had swived her months ago and like any expectant father Orkan was getting nervous as the birth approached.

The second event was that, while I sat in the Desert King's camp, I came across my bitter enemy, Zalym of the Tree Peoples (known as the Zafi). Many years ago, he had crushed my leg in battle. I still owed him keen retribution. Pilipi and I stewed under truce in the Desert King's camp, along with the bearers I led. The trek had been hard on my crippled leg. I was at the fire checking the kettle to tend to it when I felt eyes upon me.

I saw the illuminated face of the jackal when I turned from the fire. Zalym. I had no time to think of why a Zafi warrior was in the camp of the Desert King. Zalym saw my hate for him. We both reared back in surprise and instantly reached for weapons. It was only through luck I survived, for Zalym was armed with a finely polished club, while I had but the short stone knife I was using to cut cloth to poultice my leg. Nonetheless, I was faster. As Zalym raised his club to bash out my brains, I stepped in and sheathed my knife under his ribs and pushed it into his black heart.

Chaos erupted behind me. I hurried from the fire into the dark only to immediately run headlong into Pilipi, who had been fetching balm for my leg. The jar fell and shattered.

"Oh, sir," said Pilipi, "Now you have done it. That was the last balm."

Spinning him by his shoulders, I sent the slave away. "Pilipi, I have just slain Zalym of the Zafi within the camp of Orkan. Never mind the balm."

"You have broken the peace? You have slain us all! What did you do?"

"Go, gather the boars. We must fly, Pilipi! Be quick about it!"

Pilipi ran off toward Rabhana's camp. I hobbled along as quickly as I was able. I did not go directly to the queen, as one might imagine. Heading away from the campfire I sought out the tent of Gotapa, Orkan's right-hand chief, where I knew burned a rich oil lamp. The lamp burned unguarded, as all men knew Gotapa's fiery temper. I unhooked the lamp from its tripod and plucked the taper from the spout. I splashed a week's worth of oil down the row of tents. I flung the taper to set the final tent ablaze. The flame slithered away like a corn snake chasing a litter of rats. I threw Gotapa's lamp to the blaze and hurried toward the sound of squealing boars.

Queen Rabhana was already in her palanquin with the boars arrayed in the vanguard. Pilipi ran to me. He flopped my cuirass over my shoulders. He smacked my helmet onto my head hard enough to make my ears ring. "Here's your spear and shield sir!" he said, "The queen is most upset."

My boar riders stood astride their mounts.
Many a sandal was undone and cuirass yet
unbuckled, but the boars were saddled. Each
rider held his spear and wore a cheap leather version of my helm upon his head. Queen
Rabhana could be heard shrieking at her handmaid just behind the palanquin's curtain.

Without bothering with the cuirass buckles
I mounted my pig, Cicatrix. "Never mind the
queen, Pilipi," I said. I looked over my shoulder at the now-enemy camp. The flames had
spread quickly, jumping from tent to tent like
a poison frog between lily pads. Silhouettes
of men dashed around comically, frantic with
fear. The panicked rumbles of ostriches echoed
in the night. Above it all boomed the voice of
Orkan, rallying his men to douse the flames
with sand. The chaos I'd raised was amusing,
but I knew it wouldn't last long. "Up palanquin
boys! We are riding out! No need to stand on
ceremony. Daddy's kicked the hornet's nest."
I put spurs to my beast's flanks. "Scouts out!
Column forward!"

The boar, grizzled and scarred like myself,
shot forward. The tether hitched to the saddle and the palanquin's lead tautened. With a
heave, the wicker basket rocked, borne on the
backs of the boars. It moved slowly. There was
a thump inside the palanquin and the queen's
shrieking cut out abruptly.

I could hear the squeals as my men's boars
were goaded into action. Out we raced to em-

brace our friend, the night. Behind us, the camp flared bright. The gobbles of the ostriches and calls to douse the fires followed us. They had already got up a sort of shovel brigade to throw sand onto the fires. Soon the sounds faded. We were a ship sailing at night, the dunes ocean waves. The rocking of the boars calmed us.

After an hour I called a stop to rest. Dunes blocked our view of the burning camp but we still could see flickering light over the crests. The only other light was that of the stars stark overhead.

"Everyone except Kurragguz and Gau off your boars and make a tether. Leave your gourds on the saddle horn. Kurragguz, you and Gau take the passel and ride for the White River ford as fast as you can. Warn Im that Orkan is on the march."

Illi, weasel faced as usual, got down from his fat barrow, taking his gourd with him. "Leave the gourd, Illi," I ordered, "They will need all the water they can carry if they are to warn Im."

"We need to get back to Im as well, old man," replied Illi. Yet he looped the gourd's lanyard back over the saddlebow, which is all that mattered to me. He gave me a gimlet eye, "I notice you ain't climbing off your beast, now are you?"

I turned to the men, "All right, pay attention. I'm only going to say this once." I paused for a heartbeat to ensure their attention.

"We aren't heading to Im. The Hiekka are hard behind us by now. You all know how likely any one of us gets any mercy from them. We are for the forest."

Sujetan ran a hand through his perfect hair, he was the only man in the troop with every belt in place "Sir, I may be pointing out the obvious here, but the forest is away from Im." Kurnaz made side-eyes at Sujetan and nodded along.

"You think I'm an old fool. I know in which direction lies Im. It's the direction they'll least expect. Trust your elder to know a few tricks." I looked each man in the eye, one after the other. Big Garishtha with his giant club and Little Garishtha with his bow both nodded. The others shrugged and turned to their tasks.

Gau was already stringing the boars in a train. "Cut the palanquin's boars free. You boys will be carrying it." Only Illi grumbled as he shouldered the load. "I'll be scouting ahead by boar. Just keep marching and we'll make the forest by sunrise."

The morning's sun was already unbearable when we saw the forest as a line on the horizon. We were two nights past my promise. Twice we detoured around parties of Hiekka. We spotted them by the plumes of dust stirred up by their war birds at distance behind the dunes. Once a squadron of them came so close we could hear the jingle of harness, their slurred dialect, and the hooting of their mounts. We cowered in a valley of sand hop-

ing no outrider crested the dune. Disciplined
warriors all, led by an impulsive and crippled
old man.

We staggered onward toward the line. Cicatrix
plodded, his dry tongue lolling between his
tusks. We smelled rot. And growth. Water. The
men broke into a shambling trot in anticipation
of drink. The palanquin sagged under the weary
shoulders of Sujetan and Kurnaz.

I reined in Cicatrix, turned in my saddle
to look back at the dune. I wheeled the re-
luctant beast back the way we came. At the
dune, I dismounted and crawled to the crest.
The desert was alive with riders. One squadron was so near that I could see the bobbing
of their plumed helmets. Others no more than
dust rising from the horizon. The main of
Orkan's army was arrayed in a beater's line.
The nearest group of riders suddenly turned
their mounts straight to me. Rolling down the
sandpile I heaved myself into Cicatrix's saddle
and tore back toward the palanquin.

"Hop to boys! War birds are on our track. Best
we be among those trees or else we die piecemeal." The men quickened their pace, but I saw
it would be too slow. All were languid in the
heat. I held back. Giving the queen another min-
ute of liberty would be worth the sacrifice.

The rising sun silhouetted a line of war
birds along the top of the dune. Each bore
a hunched rider. Twenty or so warriors
watched—lean men, tough as the desert that

spawned them, with boiled-leather caps and breastplates, round bucklers, and stone-tipped lances. Each lance rode smartly in a stirrup bucket. Now and again the animals kicked or clawed at the sand. I could hear the creak of their saddles as warriors shifted their seats. In the middle of the flock a large warrior sat tall in the saddle—a white plume rising from his helmet. They were quite a sight.

"Keep them moving for the forest!" I ordered Sujetan. "I'll delay them as best I can."

"Don't embarrass us," said Sujetan.

I spurred Cicatrix to within shouting distance "Ho! I have come to parlay! Who leads?"

The leader was whipcord lean with a hawk's nose; his cheeks pocked with smallpox scars. He prodded his bird forward. "You know, old gimp, that it is I, Gotapa. I have come for the queen, to return Rabhana to her place. She will give birth at Orkan's side. You have broken the peace and will not be spared. Give her up peaceably and your men live as slaves."

"I cannot. Queen Rabhana is not Orkan's to keep. She is the Queen of Im and shall return there."

"You are addled in your age, cripple. Sure. Return to Im. But you are going in the wrong direction."

I shrugged.

"I'll cut the infant from her belly and leave her to bleed in the sand. She's quickened enough. The babe will live. Surrender."

84

"You have it in you today, Gotapa? Or ever? You are as squeamish around women as you are around blood. You have only love for the cloaca of your bird and your camp boys. No doubt you fear fighting me in single combat." I tried to spit. Dehydration robbed me of the desired effect. Gotapa was enraged nonetheless.

With a shriek he whipped his bird into a sprint. I sat still on Cicatrix. There could be no point in charging upslope. Every second the palanquin neared the forest. When Gotapa hit the flats, he lowered his lance and goaded his mount. The bird produced an ululating hoot. I settled my shield and spurred Cicatrix. He moved sluggishly at first, but I could tell the sight of the bird churned up something primal. The boar squealed, gathered itself and bounded forward, tusks lowered. I had just brought my spear to bear when we collided.

My breath was driven from me as I hit the sand. My wrist burned where my spear was torn away. For an unknown time all I knew was grit, white light, and pain. I rolled onto my belly to look back toward the fight. My spear stood out from the breast of Gotapa's bird, flopping rhythmically like a song-leader's wand. Gotapa was still aboard but struggling with the reins as the bird flapped and ran in a spiral. A sickening warble of pain tore at my ears.

Cicatrix was still on the move trailing intestines where Gotapa's lance had gutted

him. He ran in a wide arc back towards the
bird. Gotapa was still focused on his reins
when Cicatrix overran them both from behind. The war pig struck with his full mass,
and they tumbled in a confused array of
dust, feathers, and blood. The bird's warble
ended in an abrupt squeak. Gotapa's lance
made a rainbow arc as it tumbled across the
blue sky.

I watched the boar goring both bird and
rider, hind legs churning relentlessly. What
a terrifying pageant of aggression and pain.
When it was over, I hobbled back toward my
men.

The palanquin was nearly to the trees.
Kurnaz tripped and fell. The palanquin tumbled. The bird riders behind me charged. Each
rider yodeled in outlandish harmony with the
hooting of his bird.

The riders ignored me, converging on the
palanquin. I screamed in frustration and rage
as I saw Illi ridden under by the first rider.
Another rider fell from his bird, an arrow in
his throat. Our lone bowman, Little Garishtha,
was still within range, though I could not spot
from what hide he sent his missiles.

All I could do was watch. The birds swirled
around the palanquin, kicking up a cloud of
dust. Both Sujetan and Kurnaz were gone. The
palanquin lay on its side. A rider leaned low
from the saddle and dragged a female from
the box. I howled in despair thinking it was

the queen. But it was only her handmaid. The girl struggled in the rider's grip. She screamed as he threw her over his saddle bow. It was the rider's turn to scream when she drove a flint knife into his thigh. A spurt of bright arterial blood showed that she struck true. The man brought his club down upon the girl. Then they both tumbled from the saddle.

By then, they had the queen. There was no mistaking her gravid figure. Dismounted riders held her arms. I had failed. I was just a crippled old man whose vanity led him to accept the entourage's leadership.

It was then the giant appeared.

The arm of one of the men struggling with the queen flew off and rolled in the sand. Out of the dust a huge figure bore down the unwounded assailant. The giant easily stood two heads taller than the warrior he faced. In one hand glittered a long straight weapon such as I had never seen. The warrior let go of the queen and grabbed for the club thrust into his belt. The giant literally ran the man down. The giant's shoulder caught him in the torso. I could hear his breastbone crack even from where I stood.

Without stopping, the huge apparition loped toward the nearest warbird. The taloned kick of a bird can disembowel. The giant showed no hesitation. A flick of the strange weapon severed the bird's thin neck. The bird tumbled along with its rider. The giant impaled the downed rider with his weapon and moved on.

Three more bird riders fell in a similar fashion. It became a rout. The bird riders turned tail and ran for the desert. The giant, unable to pursue on foot, stood panting, watching the headless ostriches scrambling into one another before falling in a heap.

I walked to Gotapa. Cicatrix lay with the war bird in the stillness of death. Gotapa was pinned under the bulk of the boar. His scalp hung loose and wept blood. One eye gaped black, clotted with blood and sand.

"Yield," I said.

Gotapa stopped struggling. His chest heaved like a bellows. He spat blood and glared with the one good eye.

"I will never yield to a cripple."

I could have killed him then. I wanted to. Gotapa still had value as a hostage.

"Have it your way," I clubbed him into unconsciousness.

Leaving Gotapa, I narrowly dodged a headless bird running for the wastes. I walked back warily to the palanquin to find the strangest sight I had ever seen.

The giant kneeled before Queen Rabhana. Even kneeling, his head came up to her shoulders. He held his odd weapon before him, reversed. His head bowed, eyes downcast he raved, "Hail, holy queen, mother of mercy, hail, our life, our sweetness and our hope. To thee do we cry, poor banished children of Eve." His speech made no sense, so instead I took the man's measure. He was dressed in a woven tunic whose knits jingled with a slight sibilance at his every movement. Beneath that he wore another padded gown. Over it all, was draped a sort of white apron sewn with a red cross.

The queen stood uncomfortably. She had a streak of dirt across her nose. Pulling her cloak of feathers about her distended belly, she turned to me and snapped, "Langadi! Who is this mad giant?"

With pain I bowed to her, "I know not, my queen. He appears to have been our salvation. Best he be shown some thanks."

She nodded. "Indeed," she said. She reached out to touch the kneeling man's brow. I could see scars across his forehead as if he'd long ago been scourged with thorns. At her touch, the giant started. He reared back with a look of fear and incomprehension.

"You are our savior and among friends," she said, "Fear not."

"Holy Mary my brow burns with your most holy blessing. I am unworthy."

Rabhana cupped her tiny hands around the giant's huge fists. The hilt of his weapon stood up between them.

"Up. Rise up, mighty warrior. Have no fear. You are in our good opinion."

Shyly the giant got to his feet. Rabhana leaned in and kissed him on both cheeks.

"Come. Walk with me," she said. "I am cramped and weary of the palanquin." She walked away and the giant followed. Faintly, I could hear her exchanging meaningless pleasantries. The queen was skilled at diplomatic speech.

I felt a touch at my elbow. Trusty Pilipi. He handed me a gourd.

"Pilipi," I said, "I gave the order to give our water to Kurragguz and Gau, you know?"

"You gave that order to the men, sir. Not to me."

I took the gourd and drank deep only to gag and spit half back into the sand. It was rotgut fermented sow's milk.

"And, besides, it's not water," said Pilipi.

I gave Pilipi a sharp look, took another drink and gagged. "Well, go get someone to tie up Gotapa before he comes to. We may need him later."

Behind me, the giant man babbled, ""Blessed art thou amongst women and bless-ed is the fruit of thy womb."

I turned to look back to the queen in time to catch a slap to the face. It wasn't a strong blow but, I was still dazed from the fight with Gotapa, and it brought me to my knees. It was Kurnaz. His usual sly expression was knotted through with grief. "Sujetan is dead! This is your fault, old fool!"

Even in my current state, I knew my bold plan had taken us far from the White River and far from Im. Sujetan, not I, had paid the price. From my knees, I rapped my club across Kurnaz's shins, felling him. Then I stood. It an-gered me to see him on the ground. I brought

90

the club down upon his chest a few more times for good measure. His cuirass took the force of the blows, but the violence of the beating stunned him.

I wiped my nose and turned toward the forest. Everyone had stopped to look at us. Both Rabhana and the giant had turned back to look at the commotion. The odd giant seemed both surprised and approving. "It's best we get to the forest before they regroup. We must march."

We drank deep in the jungle. Mere steps away from the desert all became wet. Water dripped from the vegetation and sluiced us clean. The layers of desert dust on our skin first ran rich brown, then tan, and then we were clean.

Within the jungle everything was fighting. The trees fought each other for the sun. The shrubs and ferns fought for what little light filtered to the ground. Among the vegetation all manner of life was at war: cats hunted monkeys, snakes hunted rodents, rodents hunted spiders, spiders hunted flies. And, in turn the flies, rodents, and monkeys themselves fought to survive. It was like the desert. The desert, too, was a war fought for the most meager margins of life. A crumb, a drop of water, a grain of salt. The jungle was abundant. Nevertheless, all fought all. Such is life everywhere.

I hobbled along, leaning on Pilipi. The giant, who I came to realize was but a large man, insisted on helping with the queen's palanquin.

He knocked everything out of balance. Even with Kurnaz at the front, the large man took most of the load. Illi ranged far in the lead. Despite being run down by an ostrich Illi was uninjured but for the scratches raked across his face. Big and Little Garishtha, also uninjured, flanked the palanquin. Big Garishtha led Gotapa on a line. Gotapa limped along sullenly, nursing both his injuries and resentments.

Drifting from within her palanquin, I could hear Queen Rabhana chattering gaily with the giant. She told him of our city's might. How it was the only city, how the rest of the world was savagery. She described the size and lushness of our fields, spoke of her teeming citizens, how untold ranks of boar riders defended it and her, that she herself was the city.

The big man spoke too. In a hushed voice he told her he was a Frank from a land called France. France, according to him, was immense and included countless villages, towns, and cities. Cities! Plural. It still seems fanciful to me. He told of crooked streets lined with tiered homes, garrets nearly touching over the lanes, deep wells never dry even in summer. Cities surrounded by stone walls with turreted fortresses. He told of stone bridges crossing wide rivers with ferrymen poling barges underneath. On each tower flapped gaily colored pennants. Along each thoroughfare trotted haughty lords on cobs. It all seemed mad. The ravings of a lunatic. But a remarkably large and deadly lunatic that seemed to be our ally for reasons explicable only to him.

We walked with no direction. Our only goal was to disappear into the jungle, lose ourselves to the ostrich riders. Soon we were lost not only to the ostrich riders but, to ourselves. What little light reached the forest floor gave us no hint of the sun's direction. We marched on.

Near dusk we came upon a clearing. We smelled it before we saw it. The land was charred black. In the center of the cinders stood a thatched cottage on stilts and behind the cottage a series of small sheds and a fenced enclosure. Stacks of blackened coals, some still glowing, showed the inhabitants to be charcoal burners.

If there were inhabitants. We found none. "What is this place? What has happened here, Langadi?" the queen's voice carried unseen from the palanquin.

"They make charcoal here. Perhaps an accident, my queen?"

Pilipi said, "They saw us coming, put everything to the torch."

"Yes, that is it. But not all has burned."

As the men searched, I rested my leg which had become a fire. I sat in the coals and rubbed it, but the action more fanned the flames than calmed them.

"Shall we be taking our rest here, my lord?"

I looked up with a start. It was the giant. Or, rather, the man. He loomed above me. I peered up. He sensed my discomfort and, with a jingle, dropped into a squat. The tail of his white and red apron gathered cinders. It was my first good look at him. He had pulled the hood of his strange garment back. He was oddly pale with hair such as I had never seen, light and golden color. His blue eyes were also a fascinating strangeness. Yet, his jaw was strong. The wrinkles at the corners of his eyes gave him a kind look.

"We are all exhausted. We will rest a few hours then resume. At first light I'll send Kurnaz up a tree to get some bearings. Then we backtrack to the White River and Im."

"Im?"

"The queen's city."

The man looked ashamed. "I am sorry," he said. "The Holy Mother has told me a little. It seems like a wonderful place. It is only recently I came to this land. Much is confusing to me. At first, I took it for Eden, the garden. Then I heard your battle and saw the Holy Mother mishandled. I knew then it could not be Eden. Or, if Eden, an Eden beset by devils."

I shrugged, "I find I also do not know your Eden. Is it far from here? I only know a little about the geography of the Zafi."

He raised his eyes to me in surprise, "You don't know of Eden? I surely have lost my way beyond even my own limited ken. I had been told the Saracens, despite being heretics, were still a people of the book."

"These words," I said, "What book? Saracen. None of it means anything. Where in blazes do you really come from?"

The man shook his head, "You see. I don't rightly know."

He saw them as angels. The vultures circled. Waiting. Motes.

He walked. He was a knight of Christendom. Or had been. Each limping step an agony. Behind him, his track was blown to oblivion. He walked, wind at his back because it hurt less to go that way. He had long ago lost his way. He walked out of time.

Naked but for a cloth twisted about his loins and the remains of his tabard draped over his head, his skin was burned black. His sores wept thin rivulets of blood, Virgin's tears from his hands, feet, and brow. A ringlet of thorns that had once been a crown of rosebuds held the faded cloth in place.

He carried his sword like a newborn, cradled to his chest. Carried as if to preserve his life. But also, to fall upon it. This would be the worst sin. All were worms of the earth, each squirming upward for a glimpse of heaven or, more often, burrowing downward away from grace. He carried the sword like a baby.

Sand blew into his mouth. He spat but the grains stuck to his lips. The words flowed endlessly. His name, Baldwin d'Harcourt, near meaningless. The name of a love now far away—she who had gifted him with the crown of roses to wear on the peak of his helmet when he rode into battle. Battles never fought. Prester John. A task pledged and failed before it had begun. Most often, the prayer.

Áve María, grátia pléna, Dóminus técum. Benedícta tu in muliéribus, et benedíctus frúctus véntris túi, Iésus. Sáncta María, Máter Déi, óra pro nóbis peccatóribus, nunc et in hóra mórtis nóstrae. Amen. Amen. Amen.

His legs failed. Lying on his belly, eyes closed to the sand, he reached out for his sword. He found the hilt and levered himself onto his back to roll onto something hard and cool.

Baldwin opened his eyes. He was propped up against a low wall. Hardly a wall. But it did provide a break from the wind. And, blessedly, an infinitesimal shade from the sun. The row of crumbling stone disappeared into the dune. The ring around a dry well. The winds subsided. He took some solace from the abrading sand.

An angel alighted next to him. Then another. Soon, he was surrounded. Their wings beat the sand, blessing him, and edged closer. Their presence brought him peace. An angel gathered itself and moved to peck. Soon they all were working to free his soul. But his soul would not come free. Baldwin remained mired in the earth. With sudden violence the winds returned to strike the angels like waves crashing on a strand. The blow sent them tumbling back into the heavens. Still his soul would not come free. Salvation was not for him.

The wind rebuilt the dune around him. The wind must have exposed and buried this wall repeatedly. Each exposure tore particles of stone away to become the sands. Only this low wall remained. What had it been? A hut? A manor? Fort? No, look at this desert. If the stones became the desert, the desert could once have all been stone. This well once watered a great city.

Around the knight's form the sand continued to stir and build. Soon Baldwin was lost to even the keen eyes of the vultures circling where the air was clear. Then his soul came free.

He rose into the high golden dome of heaven. Through swirling mists, he heard a curious call that echoed with such insistence that it could not be ignored. He sought it out, moving through the mists by thought alone. The voice grew more distinct as he proceeded until he understood the word it spoke—it was his name that was being called across the gulfs of space and time.

The mists thinned. He saw that he was in a great golden corridor that shone near blindingly. The floor, ceiling, and walls were polished, and they were carved with the figures of ancient heroes and half-forgotten deeds: there a man clubbed a lion, a wizard turned a stick into a snake, a boy downed a giant with a stone, a snake ate its tail.

He came upon a wide stair carved of alabaster with balustrades of blooming amaranth.

The blooms dropped pollen that coated the stairs red. With each step he brushed pollen away to reveal that the steps were carved each with the abhorrent figure of Eden's old serpent. At each step he planted his heel on the head of the snake.

The voice called him on by name. At last, he came into a strange crypt. A long-bearded figure sat on a shadowed tomb. It spoke in a joyous tone.

"Oh man," it sang, "Do you know me?"

"Not I, by Heaven!" swore Baldwin.

"Man," said the ancient, "My name is John. Although my memory supplies another."

"I was sent to find you," he stammered.

"Harken!" spoke the other commandingly. "You have found me. As every windblown straw comes to rest, doings in the hidden world have brought you to me. Baldwin, the stamp of mighty happenings and great deeds is upon you. But dooms are loose. You must help the Holy Mother."

"Where is she?" asked Baldwin uneasily. He looked around. All was shining gold and amaranth dust.

"Peace!" The joyful tones reverberated through the great shining cavern. "Your destiny will be met in a city unknown to you. There you will find solace among people strange and foreign. You will meet friends and foes. Choose well between them. Gather all the people unto yourself. Pick those men in league with the evil

98

one as your enemies. All my life, I fought him. Now, in death I continue the fight. So too shall you fight for the greater glory of God. Come to me!"

On Baldwin's brow, John traced a cross of white fire with a bony finger. He felt his soul re-arranged. And in an instant crypt, mist, and gold-en dome vanished. The amaranth pollen swirled up, blinding him. For an eternity it seemed he dreamed beneath the velvet cloak of night. Then, there was a feeling, both horrific and ebullient, of a great unfolding. Born again to the world, Baldwin sprang up from a mossy sward. And as he stood, bewildered at the strangeness of his dream, he realized that he was in his harness and gripping his sword in his hand.

Then the screams began.

"Through the grace of God, I awoke into this verdant jungle. I thought myself to be in the Garden. I came to the sands to see your bold tilt with the birdmen. Then I saw them manhandle the Holy Mother from her basket."

Langadi only half heard the nonsensical tale through the throbbing of his leg.

"What is your name?"

"My name is Baldwin d'Harcourt."

"I am Langadi," I said. "You are a madman. But thank you for saving Queen Rabhana."

"Rabhana, Holy Mother, has been telling me of the city. We must get there soon as her child could come at any time."

Pilipi came running. "Oh sir, Kurnaz has been bitten by a snake!" he said, winded.

We found Kurnaz rolling on the floor of a bird pen clutching his leg. He had been rummaging among the ostrich tack when he'd been surprised by the snake. Already, a black line was moving up his calf.

"Kill me now," Kurnaz said, "It was Green Death." Rare in Im, Green Death is common in the forest. The bite leads to lingering lunacy followed by slow death.

"Hold him," I told Pilipi. Pilipi laid his body over Kurnaz's. I raised my club to brain the poor man as quickly as I could. Baldwin caught my arm, "Hold! There is another way."

"Steady his leg," said the madman. Baldwin took a length of tack and wrapped it tightly about Kurnaz's thigh.

"That will only delay the inevitable," I said.

"Perhaps. It is worth a try."

"You will only torture the man," I said.

"It will be painful. He may yet die but, I can save him from the poison at least." And, with that Baldwin took his sword and struck off Kurnaz's leg just below the knee. Crimson blood shot across the straw. None of us had ever seen such a sight. The power of his weapon awed us.

"Hold the strap tight." Baldwin tore strips from his apron to staunch the bleeding. By the time the binding was complete, Kurnaz was unconscious.

We made the queen as comfortable as could be in the hut. She bore the conditions with little complaint, but all could see that she was uncomfortable at best. Her eyes were dark circles and her whole demeanor was haggard. Graciously, she asked Baldwin to join her in the hut. "Protect me during my rest," she said. The men exchanged glances. Nothing was said.

We slung Kurnaz's unconscious form in a makeshift hammock. We tied Gotapa to a pillar under the hut. It would be uncomfortable, but such was the fate of prisoners. The rest of us slept in the cinders wrapped in what cloth could be scrounged among the compound. Our only food was a few plantains and some leather harnesses from the stables that we cut into strips and boiled to soften. Rest, at first, was fitful. I feared the charcoal burners would return.

I started awake. It was before the break of dawn. Faintly, I heard the hiss and bass hoot of an ostrich. With nudges and whispers I woke the men who silently prepared the palanquin. It was then that I came upon the severed ropes. Gotapa had escaped.

Baldwin carried the slumbering Rabhana to the wicker basket. Her oblate belly shown white in the darkness, like the moon. We strung Kurnaz's unconscious form between the handles of the palanquin. Stout Baldwin took up that load. Big and Little Garishtha took the handles at the other end. As rabbits we made our way away from the only succor we'd had since I had impetuously slain Zalym.

Upon first light I called a halt. Illi climbed the tallest tree we could find.

"What do you see?" I called up.

"Forest in all directions."

"Nothing else?"

"A little haze over there." Illi pointed.

"That's the desert that way. Anything else?"

"Some clouds over there." Illi pointed.

"Then that is the way we shall go."

Illi climbed down, blinking in the gloom of the forest.

We marched on. The men were slow and hunched. Fatigue exuded from their every pore. I dreaded being caught by enemies in the forest, weakened as we were.

We felt it first. The air changed subtly. It went from a dense mugginess to a slow churning, thin and cool. Then, the forest ended. We came into the bright sun, overlooking the verdant White River delta from a steep bluff. The bluff was a crumbling mass of eroding chalk bleeding white into the delta. We could see the lowlands cut by sinuous channels and grown with cane, fern, cattails, and moss. Mist and clouds hung above the green damp. The fens. In the hazy distance, we glimpsed the endless expanse of the sea.

"I knew it!" Maybe, I shouted a little too loud.

The men laughed in relief and slapped each other on the back. I could even hear laughter coming from the palanquin. We could see the way home. We had only to descend the bluff, cross the delta, and follow the White River upstream to Im.

I put my head into the palanquin, "My queen, we shall be home in but a day or two." She was happy but her eyes held a desperate quality, "I am glad. I have been sorely worried. I am not well."

"I think I see something," said Illi.

I turned to look at the weasel-faced man just to see an arrow lodge in his throat. He staggered backwards and then rolled down the bluff.

I didn't have to give the order.

I tackled Pilipi and together we rolled down the bluff. We landed at the muddy base with a splash, breaking our fall. We came to our feet unhurt. Baldwin and the two Garishthas grabbed the palanquin and began an awkward series of hops down the steep face. Each impact raised puffs of white dust that coated their legs. The black of the previous night's cinders made for dramatic contrast with the white of their legs. A flight of arrows sprouted from the ground where we had been standing. The palanquin was almost down. The top of the bluff now teemed with Ostrich riders. These were not the Heikka lancers but Zafi bowmen. They let loose an ineffectual volley. The arrows overshot and made sad splashes in the fen. Then, one by one, the ostriches took to the air.

Of course, the birds couldn't fly, especially with riders. For a moment I feared otherwise—it would have been an event as absurd as Baldwin's sudden appearance. But their stubby wings only slowed their fall to more manageable speeds. The bird riders made their way down the bluff in great bounds.

Everyone was already running. "Into the fens," I ordered anyway, "Be quick about it! Run!"

We waded out into the waters of the fen. Soon we were hidden in the reeds. Peering back I made out the lean figure of Gotapa on the bluff. He was pointing and shouting orders. Despite Gotapa's fury, the bird riders didn't follow far. The Zafi were not comfortable in the waters of the fen. Their birds picked up their feet as if scorched. Gotapa could not convince the riders to whip them into the milky fen.

Halfway across the delta Kurnaz became dead weight. Baldwin cut his body free. He sank into the milky bosom of the waters. Twice we had to skirt around large lizards. The first was a sinuous skink that half-walked, half-swum in the delta waters pushed along by only rear legs. The second was a long-necked brute, the size of a house dumbly grazing on cattails. We rested on the far side.

It was then I spied a pair of eyes peering at me between stalks of grass.

"Show yourself!" I shouted.

The grasses parted and a boy, skin burned brown from the sun, stepped out. Then another. And another. Soon twenty boys, all near identical stood silently before us. On each boy's back was slung a small sheaf of javelins. The first boy stepped forward.

"Don't you know me Langadi?" he said. "I am Huduga, your nephew twice removed. And, there is our queen."

I smacked my head in surprise. Of course, I knew them. These were the boys of the Scouts. Sheep herders, mostly, but also express runners and drummers. They stayed far from Im tending flocks, chasing off wolves, sending messages, searching for stray livestock. I'd never seen them as far afield as this.

"What are you doing so far from Im?" I asked.

"Looking for the queen of course, uncle. Are you rested? We must hurry." And, with that they turned and melted back into the tall grasses.

We followed as best we could, marching quickly, energized by kinfolk and the nearness of Im. As we marched, Huduga told us of how Kurragguz had ridden, mortally wounded, into the city. Before dying, he told of the queen's plight. The young Captain Anklo had taken a small force to the White River ford while the mainstay of Im's boar riders were mustering. At the ford, we found the body of Gau, pierced with arrows. He was surrounded by a make-shift barrier made from the corpses of boars. Arrayed around him lay a dozen Zafi bodies. Gau had sold his life dearly. "Never have the Zafi crossed the desert to attack Im," said Pilipi.

We all, we lucky few, knew that we would likely not see that sun rise again. The sands on the far side of the river contrasted with the grassy sward of the lands of Im. We kept the sands at bay with this grass, irrigated it with ditches and channels, seeded it as far as it would take. A generation of work now lay at risk of casual destruction. The hide tents of the besiegers dotted the sandy plain. Our small troop would be insufficient to successfully dispute the crossing of the river, outnumbered as we were. Orkan had not dared march on to Im with this rump force at his back. So overnight he had sent his ostrich riders to the dispersed desert camps to rally the greater bulk of his footmen to join his Zafi allies. Now, the mass of their combined infantry had gathered to contest the ford. I could not count their warriors. Nor could Pilipi. Several thousand at least.

Later, I heard a cry from the palanquin.

"Sir! Sir!" cried Pilipi, "The queen's waters have given way. The baby is coming."

It was decided. The queen could no longer travel. We would have to follow Gau's example. We would try to hold the ford and hope the scouts would bring relief from Im.

We formed a shield wall on the low bank of the ford. The few archers I put under Little Garishtha's command. Anklo, the young guard captain, led the remainder of the fighting men. He was pitifully green and our line was uncomfortably thin.

"Do you think a fighting retreat might work?" Anklo looked pale and concerned.

"We would be surrounded and destroyed. Here is our killing ground." I looked sharply into the young man's eye. He had to know there was no hope of retreating. "Here! We kill until we die!"

The horns sounded. The enemy ranks drew up. They were armored in boiled bull hide. Before the massed infantry rode a troop of ostrich riders. Skirmishers moved in serpentine patterns. Occasionally, one would loose an arrow across the ford. A slow drizzle of harassing missiles mostly fell short but, enough landed among the men to keep their attention and shields in place. On each wing, troops of heavier ostrich riders flocked. Each man wore a plumed helmet, breastplate and carrying a lance.

Side-by-side in the middle the Hiekka's sun banner rose beside the Zafi's cow-skull totem. It seemed an alien alliance, unclean. Looking at this dire sign, I knew an even greater love for Im, the land beyond the White River. I could make out the large, lethal figure of Orkan, surrounded by his guard, and even the lean snake of Gotapa—now wearing an eye patch. To Orkan's flank was a profile that made the bravest blanch—the squat figure of Malimo, King of the Zafi. He stood a head taller and twice as wide as any warrior on the field. The toad-like man leaned on an obsidian studded club that came to his shoulder. To see such in the company of

Orkan was a hard blow to our understanding of the world. The desert folk had always been deadly enemies of the forest folk. No longer. The men began to murmur in dread.

The skirmisher birds suddenly trotted off to the wings. The spearmen moved forward, toward the turbid, chalky waters of the White River; the ostrich riders cantered forward, lances lifted, plumes streaming. Quite a sight. Our warriors drew a tired breath and wiped the sweat from their palms for better grip on their spears. I saw that Baldwin had acquired a leather helmet to sit atop his metal hood. He had scrounged up a round buckler for his free hand. He also held his terrible weapon, which gleamed brightly in the sun. As one, the enemy began a simple chant, "Kill! Kill! Kill!"

I clapped Anklo on the shoulder and smiled. "You hear? All is clear now. We mean to kill them, and they us. Have no fear! We shall see these dogs off. The water shall hinder them." Anklo gulped and said nothing. But something chilled me in spite of this glorious moment. Beneath the sound of maneuver, I could dimly make out an occasional animal cry. It came in a sharp series. Queen Rabhana locked in her birthing throes.

As they marched, the approaching men struck their spears against their shields. The horns blew again. The enemies paused at the milky waters. For a moment, silence prevailed. Then, an order was given. They gave a huge roar and charged down the bank, into the milky flood. The water foamed up to their thighs. An occasional warrior tripped on a hidden obstacle, perhaps a corpse felled by Grau in his previous battle. Something disrupted and slowed the approaching formation, anyway. A few of these men failed to gain their feet and were trod under only to surface again downstream.

On the downstream flank a troop of bird riders half-waded, half-swam to outflank us. Their goads overcame the bird's natural mistrust for water. "Little Garishtha! Take your archers and pincushion those birds. Ignore the riders." The archer and his twenty men took off at a jog toward the downstream flank. Soon after, I heard the squawk of wounded fowl. But I had no time to evaluate the small archer's efficacy as the enemy foot was now much closer.

"Anklo, this is a good time for the javelins." The young man nodded and turned to his men arrayed on the bank.

"Javelins forward! Throw all you've got then move behind the shield wall!" From between the shield men the javelin boys emerged, Huduga in their lead. Each boy wore nothing but a loincloth. Each carried three slim darts. They threw the first volley as a group. At such close range against a massed target it was impossible to miss. Many of the missiles glanced off helmets and breastplates or thudded into shields. Just as many struck into exposed thighs and arms. I saw one man fall with a shaft protruding from his open mouth. They were swept away by the flood. The front ranks faltered as the boys began throwing their second missiles piecemeal. More men fell. The upstream flank became disordered as fallen men tripped up their neighbors. For a moment I thought the wavering group might break and fall back across the river. The boys expended their missiles and quickly withdrew. The enraged infantry hit the riverbank. To their credit they maintained their cadence of, "Kill! Kill! Kill!"

The bank was only a few steps above the waters. This was advantage enough. Our front rank could put their spears into the first men. Nearly all of these died. But the weight of men behind, desperate to leave the water, pushed the dead forward onto them. The shield wall held firm, the men thrusting underhanded recalled the remorseless thrusting of a boar's loins as it mounted a sow. The air was full of screams, and lieutenants' orders. "Stand firm! Hold fast! Strike fast!" Still, the enemy pushed forward. New spears met them.

One of our front rank was yanked from formation—literally rooted out by bleeding men who pulled him up by his shield and passed him back overhead. We heard him being slaughtered by those behind. "Baldwin, follow me," I shouted, but was betrayed by my game leg. Baldwin had already charged forward into the gap. The weapon lashed out to pierce a leather breastplate. Baldwin kicked the screaming warrior off his blade and swung again to shear off a man's ear and jaw. By the time I reached the fight, I had lost all sense of what was happening. It was a ceaseless pushing against the relentless mass. I thrust my spear into it time after time. I don't remember losing my weapon but only that there was a time when I was swinging my club into the enemy helmets, shoulders, and faces. I sprawled forward and rolled down the bank to the river. The enemy had broken and were splashing back to their displeased leaders. I sat in the shallows and laughed.

Pilipi hauled me back up the bank and over a heap of dead bodies, "It's the queen, sir. You'd better come." I pushed my way through our re-forming shield wall. At a rough guess, maybe a quarter of our men were out of the fight, wounded or killed. Rabhana had been moved from her palanquin to a tent. The leather flap was closed and outside stood Big Garishtha on guard with a look of shocked horror on his face.

"She's bleeding, sir. I don't know what to do." The big man was literally wringing his hands in worry. I'd seen him open a man and laugh as his adversary ran across a meadow trailing his guts but, now the sight of a woman's blood paled him.

"Go to the fight," I ordered the large warrior, "You can do more there in any case." With a look of profound relief Big Garishtha hurried to the shield wall. Doubtless, he preferred his own impending death to this responsibility. "Pilipi, gather whatever cloth or batting you can find."

Rabhana lay within the tent. She was naked and lay on her ruined cloak of feathers, now black with blood. In the dimness of the tent her skin shone thick with sweat and grime. Her eyes caught mine with a desperate look, "Langadi, I'm so weak. Help me. I'm bleeding," then she convulsed with pain and shrieked. Her majesty had been reduced to animal instinct by the throes of labor.

"I will help you," I said. There was little to do but hold her hand and wait for Pilipi to return. And again, I lost my sense of time. All was shrieking and soothing, sopping up blood with soiled cloths, and telling the woman, once a queen, to push. I barely noticed that outside the battle had resumed without me. The rhythm of Rabhana's screams seemed to rise and fall with what sounds of conflict penetrated the tent.

A hand was striking at my shoulder, "Sir! Sir," it was Pilipi, "You'd best come!"

"I am busy Pilipi."

"Come now! I fear we are lost." Looking up, Pilipi's normally unflappable face showed creases of concern. I got up and grabbed Pilipi's shoulders to look him sternly in the eye. "Pay attention. Stay with her. Help."

Outside the tent, all was chaos. In all directions men were in savage conflict. The shield wall was being turned. By main force, our line was being rocked back to form an arc that would soon join into a circle. What groups of warriors who had broken from the main body were now surrounded and forlorn.

I picked up a dropped spear and walked toward our line. In the center, near the enfeebled shield wall I saw the sun banner and the skull totem rise. The leaders had joined the fight. I could hear Anklo rallying the men "To me! To me! Steady!" he cried. Big Garishtha was at his side, covering the young leader with his shield while he struck with his club.

But where was Baldwin?

The Zafi shrieked and thrust their spears at an isolated group. Within the whirling dust Baldwin dashing, striking, and dodging. From inside the dust I could hear his cry, *"Deus Vult! Deus Vult!"* Baldwin seemed protected by his mail. His crossed apron was in tatters. A few arrows snagged in the cloth flapped along with him. I was sure that soon, despite his armor, he'd be borne down by sheer numbers. I ran to him.

The nearest forest person, a squat brute of a man with ear disks the size of dinner plates, was so focused on Baldwin that he did not notice my approach until my spear emerged from his chest. The weapon was dragged from my hands as the man fell. I laughed at the dying man's foolish expression and ducked just in time to avoid the club of his brother. I tackled him. We rolled in the dirt, both consumed by animal fear, rage, and lust for the other's death.

My opponent seemed nothing but a ball of coiled muscle. I held him close around the waist. He pounded my back with his club, but the angle weakened his blows. I'd be bruised but my breastplate meant the blows were not lethal. As we rolled, my hand landed on the hilt of a knife the warrior had tucked into his girdle at the small of his back. I tore the knife free and drove it into his unarmored back again and again.

Out of the dust Baldwin stepped forward to offer me his hand. "Out of the fight already?" he asked. "Stand up. We must go relieve Anklo." He hauled me to my feet. He took off at a run to join our line. I hobbled after. We entered the line just as it closed into a circle. We were surrounded but together.

Again, it was a time of heaving and pushing. I had no weapon. The best I could do was grab a lost shield and push back with whatever remaining force I had. Our shield wall held. When a man fell, we stepped in, and closed ranks. Our circle grew smaller. Step by step we were pushed back down the riverbank. I pushed with my shield but could feel myself giving ground. The waters lapped at my ankles.

A horn blew. In an instant the enemy withdrew. The sudden absence of resistance caused me to stumble. We looked about, dazed. We saw a plumed array of bird riders, lances leveled. The horn blew again. They charged. The birds closed with incredible speed. Just before impact every other bird took to the air in an awkward, flapping leap. The remaining riders

114

reached us just as the jumping birds landed amid our circle to strike randomly with their lances. The man next to me was impaled through the cheek by a lance. As he rode by, the rider heaved his lance skyward, flipping the man through the air in an arc like a fisherman landing a hooked fish. Then I was struck and sent sprawling into the river.

The effect of the charge was devastating. It broke us. Men fled, splashing into the river. I tripped and stumbled through the murk with them. Fortunately, neither the lancers nor the infantry followed. Soon we had reformed into a smaller circle. The water was up to our loins. We were unsteady in the water.

I joined Anklo, Baldwin, and Big Garishtha. Anklo was bleeding from a cut across his face. As usual, Big Garishtha seemed untouched although his chest heaved. The giant Baldwin was our center. Arrayed in his strange armor Baldwin's sheer alienness had become a comfort. We made for less than a quarter of our original strength. We huddled together in the cool flow. The men dipped their helmets to drink from the river. I did the same.

We could see the enemy ranks forming up on the shore. There was Orkan with his sun banner. His ostrich riders were running in circles raising dust. The bass rumbles of the birds carried to us across the water. There was Malimo at the front of a body of the Zafi.

"What do we do grandfather?" asked Anklo. I was taken aback by the honorific. "We stand and die and take as many as we can with us." I shrugged. "We do as before." The young man seemed startled, even disappointed. No doubt I was too curt. Anklo gathered himself. He sighed.

"Yes, that is all that's left."

"How is the queen?" asked Big Garishtha.

"I do not know. She is with Pilipi. She may be captured."

The big man looked disheartened and I felt a pang of guilt. After all, I had left a bleeding woman in her hour of need. A silence passed among us.

"We will pray," said Baldwin. He raised his weapon to the sky, hilt up and recited the words, "*Áve María, grátia plena...*" The words had no meaning to me, but he recited them with such conviction that we found ourselves heartened, if only by joining our voices to his. Whatever the words meant, Baldwin was certain they would help us in some inexplicable way. We heard the horns sound again and turned back to look at the shore.

At the tip of the rough wedge Malimo roared his heathen battle-cry and swung his great club in broad arcs. He strode straight at our line, the forest dwellers close behind. The cow-skull totem bobbed behind his shoulder, borne by a chosen warrior. We surged forward mimicking their battle cry, "Kill! Kill! Kill!" There was no feeling that the battle hung in balance, for we had already given up hope of

116

victory. But there was still opportunity to hurt our enemy.

Big Garishtha left our ranks to meet Malimo. Neither faltered as they waded toward one another. Malimo swung his club and Big Garishtha caught it on his shield. Malimo had the reach on him though and Big Garishtha could not bring his own club to bear. Time after time the obsidian studded club struck the warrior's shield. There was no finesse, just brute strength. Finally, the club thudded down and we heard Big Garishtha's arm give way like a green twig snapping. With a shout of pain, the warrior dropped the shield. And that was that. Malimo swung his club into the side of Big Garishtha's head and the unstoppable warrior was swept away by the river.

Malimo struck down thunderbolts, hurtling through our ranks by sheer power, striding against the current of the river. Soon the waters around us all took on a pinkish cast. Malimo splashed through our ranks and none could stand against him.

Malimo was half as wide as he was tall with a belly like a cannibal's cauldron. He waddled toward Baldwin. His silver weapon lashed out and struck the totem bearer's head from his shoulders. The totem, also beheaded in the same stroke, fell and vanished into the milky water. Malimo swung his club in a wide defensive arc. Baldwin was struck in the ribs. For the first time I saw Baldwin stagger. He dropped his famous weapon. It slid smoothly into the water and disappeared.

Malimo cheered when he saw his foe falter. He lashed out wildly with his huge club. It thudded dully on the knight's helmet. Baldwin staggered. For a moment he seemed dazed. He looked at his empty hands. Malimo, too, was taken in by this confusion and tried to find the object for which Baldwin was looking. It was then that Baldwin leaped. For perhaps the first time in his life, the giant king lost his footing and fell.

Malimo's tree-trunk arms flailed ineffectually. The huge feet kicked to no avail. The two giants rolled in the waters. They raised a great spray. Finally, they both disappeared beneath the surface. Baldwin came up; Malimo did not.

The Zafi stopped fighting, searching from the banks for their king. One by one and in small groups they crossed upstream of us and walked back to the desert. They ululated and yipped as they went. Some of our scouts still had the energy to lob spears at their backs. I thought of ordering them to desist, lest a rage rise in them. But I was too exhausted to care. I watched Baldwin diving to retrieve his lost weapon.

Orkan was shouting and gesticulating to the Hiekka. His men formed up and began a slow march toward us. A horn sounded, not their vulgar cow horn—but the deep clay horns of Im. On the low hillock stood arrayed the boar lancers of Im. The riders wore helmets with boar-bristle crests. The horns of Im resounded across the river, this time a shrill note that tailed off with a warbling cry. And with a squeal, they charged.

Orkan tried desperately to wheel his men to face the war pigs but it was too late. The heavy boars struck their flank and swept through them like a river breaking a levy. The great sun banner of the Hiekka fell from view. The defenders of Im, exhausted and enraged from the desperate ride from Im, struck down the fleeing men without mercy. Some warriors, who had been chased downstream, threw themselves into the river to drown in their armor.

I felt no exaltation. The change in our fortunes had been too sudden. I scaled the embankment of dead bodies for the third time that day. The sun was not yet low on the horizon but, already the corpse flies had appeared. All about me were the bodies of men and birds, with few boars among them. I saw Little Garishtha, bearing his bow, retrieving arrows with his few remaining archers.

I went to the queen's tent. As I approached, I heard another scream. Pilipi, red to the elbows, emerged bearing a bundle swaddled in bloody linen on his arm. He still held a stone knife in his off hand.

"The queen?"

"She is no more," the slave sighed.

I peered at the babe. "The child is well?"

"I believe so, sir. He will need food, soon. A wet nurse."

Beyond Pilipi, Rabhana lay motionless in disarray. Her once distended belly was deflated and rent with the wound that rescued her son. She seemed older. That is, in death, she seemed older. The young maiden, briefly a mother, had become a crone. I wrapped her as best I was able with the remnants of her feathered cloak.

When I emerged, Pilipi was sitting in the dust with his head in his hands. He shook. His knife was in the dirt. At his side stood Baldwin with the babe in his arms. He dandled the child, who suckled on his blood-encrusted finger.

"Rabhana is no more?" asked Baldwin.

"She is dead," I said.

"She has entered heaven. She has found peace. I have no doubt."

I had no reply. I looked out to the field of battle. All I could see was dead men with wounds in their backs. Dead men locked into each other's embrace, like lovers. Dead men pierced by spears, arrows, lances. Dead men, with skulls crushed by clubs, features horrifically distorted. Dead men on their way downstream.

We went on.

Only Little Garishtha, Pilipi, and I lived of our original party. Of Anklos's command but a score survived. Miraculously, none of the boys had been killed—or even injured. Wisely, they had all run off after casting their darts.

Later, I found Gotapa, a broken lance thrust through his throat. It angered me that the battle was such that we never came to grips. We never found Orkan.

In later years, at the corners of oxbows, there came to be sandbars made of bones.

Our own dead, we gathered up to carry on boars back to Im and their families. The carrion birds circled the field as our column turned for Im. Baldwin watched the skies.

"The angels are gathering," said Baldwin.

When we sighted Im, I could tell that the city did not rise to Baldwin's image. No tiered and garretted rooftops, no ferrymen poling barges, no tall fortress. No pennants at all. No grand bridge crossing a grand river. Baldwin saw no haughty lords trotting on horseback through the thoroughfares.

The river was more a brook. The wall was but a loose wooden palisade woven with thorns rather than reinforced with stone. My home was hovels of low, rectilinear brick made of clay, straw, and dung. Baldwin's tales of France had changed something in my old eyes. Im stood in a haze of smoke from dried pig dung burning in crude grates. Even from afar, it smelt of the leavings with which we fertilized everything. Baldwin stopped and took it all in.

"Well, it's a start," he said.

And so this was how we came to lose our queen and gain a king. Baldwin placed Rabhana in the basket of her palanquin along with wood and tinder. We set the makeshift boat afloat on the White River. The whole of the city came out to watch our former queen drift away aflame.

We dragged the ford in search of Baldwin's weapon, but it was never recovered. As the decades passed, the white river's milky waters shifted to form a new ford leaving behind what came to be called Queen's Lake. Some of the poorer and more ignorant farmers see ghosts on the waters. Rabhana, they say, can be seen beneath the surface, burning with cold flame, cradling the weapon in her arms, like the child she never held. I do not say it is only the moon.

Baldwin was a good and wise ruler. He knew much and taught us lore such as we never knew. He fought like a drowning man to better the city. Many evenings I would bid him goodnight while he sat at his table poring over scrolls only to find him still at his table come morning. Under his rule we expanded the territory to include the whole river valley, from the delta of the White River, east and west to the mountains south to where the river widened into marshes. I accompanied Baldwin, riding my boar at his side, in all this doing. It took time, but eventually even the Hiekka and the Zafi became the people of Im. The child, named Nimrod, became Baldwin's heir. Baldwin taught us of his three-fold god. Many of the city folk swear by it today. But I must confess I never understood it. To me there is only mud, water, fire, the winds, offences, retributions, life, and death. Death claims us all.

My joints came to ache and my crippled leg throbs continuously. I stay home. Grandfather that I am, I never expected to outlive Baldwin. I did though. One day, Baldwin was out hunting in the White River fens. A lizard surprised him, charging out of the tall grasses. The beast grabbed him and dragged him out to deep water. The giant man's strength had waned. By the time his huntsmen had slain the beast, our king was drowned. And, so Nimrod, now grown, became king.

Im grows under the rule of Nimrod. Just as I expected to die in battle and to precede Baldwin, I am twice surprised. Nimrod talks of plans to construct a strong tower of stone from which to survey the whole of Im's territory. He speaks of priests crying the prayers in all the languages of Im: city, desert, forest, and more to come.

I am brought low by time. Baldwin's story of the angels and his walk in the desert stays with me. I am like the stones, scoured away by the sea of sand, diminishing, to be buried and forgotten.

ELEKTRA AND THE LAWS

Norberto Argentavis
translation by Neal Durando

She began under spoiled thatch, matted into sheets, some gone fragrant, shot through with a rot which yellowed what rain would pass. Her mother had, summers, matted it together, confused with rushes and sage. It was then, perhaps, the girl mixed this smell together with that of herself. She watched her mother sitting in sunlight on a stool within a golden whirl of motes, embracing then wrangling the thatch together. The girl was warm then cold and then had to be unwound herself. Her mother did this also. The man there, her father, was good about the day, but lazy about the season. He left the ladder by and so much undone besides. They would find the ladder still standing at the eaves. Her mother wound her in a bundle. He climbed to the roof, rustled and stomped in the rafters, reset the thatching until it no longer leaked. This man did not go out in the rain or much of anywhere by morning. He failed to repair the cob wall but they liked the air. He sat by the fire for long hours, his hair rising in the warmth. Then the baby had croup. She cannot recall her brother, where he was, his caprices, what noises he made. They unwound the baby together. He was noisy. They burned a bit of thatch in the hearth and blew sparks and cinders in the baby's face. He whooped. The catarrh could not in this way be dislodged. Together they watched the fire. Her mother tied the shutters tight when the latch came free and could not be again driven into the cob. There came such winds which blew their hearth red.

Her father was always on his way outside, and once there walking, disturbed and searching, disturbing heaps and middens with an iron poker, muttering. His bottles and other discoveries tipped over with a rattle. They consumed too much wood. In the cob wall there was set a stone shaped like an owl, which sheer fancy made her friend. They burned what her father pulled from the middens. Pallet wood, magazines, powder which roared to life when thrown in the fire, one time an old doll. Her father was always rising from his hearth-side stool to tempt the weather. He taught her to stoke the fire in his absence.

He plowed, she supposed, although she cannot recall any notion of a horse. Or gathered or killed. Somehow, they ate. They watched for the airship through a cracked shutter and did not go outside. The man returned his burdens to the flames. Her mother was about her mysterious affairs, the knives, her brother. He brought in wet wood. They ate hot broth brewed from the bones of the ox. He brought back the bottles that he found in the middens. He carried them in a basket which rattled. "Don't worry," he said, " It is only broken glass." He brought in boards, bowed and wavy and sodden. She saw how they were composed of pressed dust. "Because it is not wood," he said, " See?" He could tear them apart with his hands easy as books. In the guttering, late, the stones around the owl assumed the shape of airships and grenades. His bottles hissed and spewed and made him laugh and then curse "Hot Skiboo!" He brought back a cough which everyone caught but the boy, whose coughing days were over. Her father cleaned his mouth on his sleeve. The rooms filled with smoke. She worried a hole in her wrist with her thumb and so was assured of her own presence, that she had not been dispersed to the winds.

And when, in Elektra's memory, the chimney caught fire they went out from that place but did not immediately leave. They watched it burn from beneath an oak. She did not remember when they had all been outside at once. This did not attract an airship, although her mother caressed her head and watched the heavens. They watched as the door was drawn inward on its hinge, as if some specter were setting up behind it to surprise a child.

Her mother coughed. A cloud came out. The cob house panted before it settled to the clay with animal effort. It blew up a ball of fire which broke apart the chimney pots, upset the ladder from the eaves, and cast a brief shadow upon the court. Fire casts a shadow. This was not lost on Elektra. In her memory, the old ox blew blood from its muzzle after the hammer. The spray hung in the air like indecisive bees after the beast went to its knees. Only this spray caught fire and snarled away to nothing. The crack in the cob wall widened and grew from the eaves to the sills. What powers had her father concealed within their home? Where did her mother hide her knives?

Her mother would not stop coughing. The owl came free, tumbled into the fire like a stone, no longer anyone's friend. The roof wheeled and fell, following the walls. The thatch, strangely, did not blaze but elaborated a fulsome bonnet of smoke instead, which did not immediately disperse.

In Elektra's memory she blew the seeds from a dried pee-a-bed. Such was her experience with explosions. Soft flurries of brief warmth. What she retained. The wet crescendo of the falling beast. Elektra retained what she could touch. The groan of the cob wall's sudden collapse. She watched the thatch smolder. Straws and hanks of it rose in a fashion that put her in mind of her father's hair. It was all very hard to put in proper order. Her father's hair over the long moments when he withdrew within himself at day's end, his boots to the hearth, wet and brimming with stink, his matted locks drying. All this and more Elektra would contain. It was only a cob house on fire. It was only water. It was only ash. Her mother, in memory, then ceased to appear along with the boy. What would fill her now? Elektra wondered.

Or the oak was not before the house. Or it was another one, an alder, farther out, by the older middens. She was struck—they all were— by the sight of the preceptors and their batmen arrayed there in a black rank. The scavenger, her father, stepped out from the shade, as if searching the furrows where the turf became muddled into the apron of the carriageway. His boot could not scuff or bother its golden circuits, though he tried. Some demon force within resisted whatever he could kick up. Her father's eyes did not leave the ruts, as if he would lose his way back beneath the sod should he ever look away. Was it at this moment Elektra's suspicions began? Her father was not worried about the strange presence of the preceptors, silent in their cloaks, he was already making plans to dig a new house for three.

This rescue oak marked a budgetary set-aside, an outstation, the presence of the tree marked it easily visible from airship. Her father wedged his feet into the ruts. He spoke only when he could go no further. "Receive Elektra," said her father, in memory, his hand hard to her back. "Give her work." The father's voice became gradually laden with a great burden. The heavy effort he made to speak made his voice strange to himself and grew more onerous with every word. What he said she does not recall so well. The carriageway was electric, indifferent to the weather, and made a slight vibration through one's shoe. "See she's fed," he said as if speaking while setting his knees to displace a boundary stone. A tall preceptor produced a clever shovel, which unfolded in his hand with a series of oily clicks. Her father barely dared to step forward and grasp it in the middle of the haft. His last word ended in a squeal delivered with a homeward turn. She was not entirely sure she had caught it. He did seem diminished. This was it. Nobody was coming to help. The man had his shovel. But Elektra decided then she would rather retain her father's hair rising in the red draft, to contain the sight forever. Evenings at the hearth. The wisps and motes rose and settled into a place within her.

❋

The preceptor, the most upright one, spoke in a soft pressing voice that made one strain all the harder to hear.

"Immediate departure," he said.

Does he mean me? Elektra wondered. What do I do? He wore long sleeves wound with embroidered laws and amulets. Where does he want me to go? Away? His face was painted with a faint smile and setting sunlight. Immediate departure, she supposed, might be the best that could be expected. The others broke their rank. She was taken by the arm, relieved not to have been singled out or dismissed. She would have done anything in that moment, she realized later, recalling this place in the mud. Whenever the heat of a fire tightened across her face, when leaves whorled a certain way on the breeze—even distant birds could do the trick, should they scatter a certain way, startled from a field of stubble—or when watching the evening motes and flies rising in the long October light, Elektra would come unrooted from wherever she was to return to this oak.

"So, we are to travel to the city," decided Ilea Lark Urkl, "Or so I suppose." The crone clutched to her arm for support. They were still standing in the mud. Her father had gone away to memory. They had come for a girl at the rescue oak and here she was, unnamed to anyone but her own, beyond registry. The

crone clutched to the girl or the girl guided
the unsteady woman in thick shoes. They went
along, both independent or in flight, caught or
bending to the bush, somehow now insepara-
ble. The air within the articulated whined. The
place smelled sharp.

"I am not from the city," said the girl. Ilea
Lark Urkl would not detach. She had a moist
hold on Elektra as if she were a bit of sodden
dough in want of flour. For her part, the crone's
face was a whole fallen loaf, dry in spots, with
a rosy net of wrinkles, tumors, and cracks laid
across, something spent, which no amount of
yeast could revive. Elektra looked down to her
elbow but not beyond, her head tilted as if to
listen. She did not think of her mother baking,
nor where her mother hid her knives in the
house. She instead thought of something which
would be discovered living under punk wood,
quivering with corruption. She instead thought
of a knife baked into a loaf. Together they
crossed a burnished companionway. The articulated grew large enough around them that, for
an instant, Elektra imagined herself outside.

"Nobody is not from the city," said Ilea Lark
Urkl. Like the others she wore a cloak trimmed
in fur. Her sleeves were also wound with silk-
en laws and rods of black glass.

"I have never been there," said Elektra. They
entered what would be her berth. A plush ap-
pointment, a picture porthole, a mesh as tall as
a butler, a banquette, and recamier.

"We are already here," said the crone. "We turn forever inward. We walk away together. We seed hay everywhere. We climb the hill. Or so it is said." The crone settled onto a divan. "We," intoned Ilea Lark Urkl, "are the flame of the breath that put God in the earth. We set out for foundlings at rescue oaks." The effect of this incantation was limited to Elektra deciding the tree could not have been an alder. The old woman's claw traced a circle in the air. "We are the ones who draw red lines around things."

The girl could think of nothing to say. She scratched open the scab on her wrist. A page appeared at the door. The girl was presented with a blanket and a cup.

"Draw the curtain away, girl," said Ilea Lark Urkl, indicating the porthole. And so Elektra realized they were already at speed and gaining on the carriageway, traveling beyond any notion of her father. Swales filled with wild krop. Tracks. Horizons of red lumps of seized machinery, rusting. A ramble of a wooden pen that would have been easy to dismantle, stack, and burn. Across such distance it was hard to say with any certainty what was big or close.

"What is your name?" said Ilea Lark Urkl after a while.

"Just so," said Ilea Lark Urkl after it became clear Elektra would hold her peace, "We will speak of it later."

When Elektra woke, she found the first preceptor was bent to Ilea Lark Urkl, who had not moved from the divan. The crone's feet dangled just above the floor, under which played a soft jazz of speed.

"We haven't the margins to teach her sticks and stones and electric flux," said the man. "Cleanliness. Better words. A bare minimum."

"We may have to begin again," said Ilea Lark Urkl with an amused air. "Forthrightness. She is stubborn. I suspect she is now feigning sleep." The crone let out a shriek, which she bent to the color of a laugh. "I'll get her to dance atop a pole and recite the usurpers in reverse order. Whatever is your will. Then she will speak. Maybe before. Fit for purpose. And never out of turn."

Elektra arose, redressed herself upon the recamier, drew her blanket tight about her.

"Instead," said the man regarding the girl, warmly amused with the confirmation of her deception. He addressed the crone while Elektra watched him through one eye. "Why don't you entrust her with something small to comfort and protect. Toss together some rags and swizzles. Perhaps a small animal she might feed cake or seed." His hand now soared out. The gesture was made for Elektra. The preceptor winked. "Maybe denature a one-way bird? Erase its capacity for advanced speech? Lure out a rat? I don't know." The smiling preceptor bent over her and put out his hand as one did to a dog.

❁

"Did Ilea Lark Urkl not say that I am called Jon Hauk Or?" he said. The girl stood upon a Persian carpet.

Although now the subject of direct attention, the Elektra was flown far away, well beyond reception. Even the crone's shriek and cackle emitted upon tumbling back to the divan, amusement after failing to rise under her own power, could not call Elektra back. The girl sat at the porthole, put her chin to the brass fitting and the world full of iron and retention pools and stumps. So she could also see the sky from the recamier, she had again taken up residence in the sore on her wrist, the scar of which she worried apart in every dry season. She woke the weeping dimple, her red home.

Now, Elektra could see herself standing, about to alight in the articulated, for a far remove, just moments ago, as if circling on silent wings. Her trousers were faintly streaked with blood from where she had drawn the sore across her legs, absently. She had grown distant again, ever her father's daughter. Her mother was both scolding and absent, the one who had first opened the wound on her arm, with a tiny clasp knife. Jon Hauk Or had gone when she looked again.

The mesh danced like a fire, never growing constant, every time it caught the light from the metallic surface of a passing retention pool. Her sore gave her hand somewhere to go, a pang that centered her body in space, whenever the dominant hand wandered off to find the weaker.

A warmth welled up within her, lengthened and stiffened, becoming a hot wire running through her diaphragm. She tried to stifle this welling. Tightening her stomach only made it more acute. Elektra coughed up a spark. It brimmed out, grizzling over her teeth, settling into her lap an inert jewel. She jumped when it suddenly stirred to life, escaping outwardly at speed without diminishing in intensity.

Her surprise took a moment to swallow, confirm, believe. The spark had felt bigger on the inside and had apparently passed through the pane. She put her forehead to the glass and could watch its bright streak until the articulated turned it from her view. Could such things, she wondered, really come to pass absent independent witness, absent a brother to exclaim, "What in creation was that?!"

The mesh continued its ambient dance in the corner but it was not alive. Who would know—who could tally—aside from her? Just what was a girl to suppose? I felt it pour through me, she thought. Something did tick over in my heart. My true name is Elektra, as everyone probably knows. I wear no law on my sleeve. Sometimes my hand drops dead. And do I not also bleed? I should speak with

Jon Hauk Or, she thought, he will know. I do not trust this crone. How long am I to be left to her. Until she wins?

And, left alone, the girl removed her clogs. She put her cheek to the brass fitting of the porthole again. She looked out fearful that she would recognize the land, fearful of sighting of her mother on the downs, or else being drawn back to her former self by a shot-out steeple or a tumbled stack. She was terrified, transfixed, that what she sees will not be new or unknown. This froze her to her porthole, would weld her thumb to her wrist until the reached the city proper.

The carriageway had widened. Figures she imagined to be mysterians strode the upper promenades, disinterested in the passage of the articulated. She found herself deeply nested into the recamier, unable to simply remain perched in such a yielding place. No barefoot escape she might make from the berth would ever be quick. Elektra did not want to dirty the velour. She allowed the cushions to come up around her until the articulated set itself into a lazy curve and, of a sudden, the way ahead was revealed.

Elektra wondered at the long bundles of sodden, black laundry suspended from the light masts. She winced when the boots of the dead began to kick at the vehicle's roof. Their drizzle became a terrible roar. She did not quit the recamier. Liberated boots and limbs skittered to the apron. Elektra bowed her head but did not give in to her instinct for the floor. Who desired this? the girl wondered. I am inside a very wicked place. Or else the laws are most severe, indeed. Why?

She raised her eyes once the articulated again adopted a straight course. An expanse of catchment pools cast up a weak chemical glow. By their light multiplied there was nothing to see but further catchment pools, further fluorescent wallows, sludge wherein dark booms turned sludge slowly onward. We have always been inside the city, thought Elektra, even though it did not seem so.

Already she has never been this far away. She had never seen or imagined these channels and basins and scrap yards and sumps, the stacks of reinforcing material, cladding, the foam reservoirs, the automatic lathes laboring unattended in weather sheds. She began to discern there had once been a city here, or that there would be one soon again. The ordered arrangement of the ruin was too congested to take in at speed viewed from the carriageway. It was simply too much.

They flew by sundered hangars, bunkered salt and sand, a tarmac strewn with sunbleached fuselages, too expansive for the available light. Elektra let her eye wander into the outer dark along the graceful arcs of their white wings. Small movements brought it back from these discarded angels into the sickly green-white illumination accumulated around the heaps. She saw something of herself in the headless servitors who blackened the failed layer cakes of ferrocrete slabs, lying perturbed as if flung about by a disturbed baker, bees upon their remotely orchestrated errands. Elektra, cannot at this distance and speed, determine whether they are animal or machine. She had never imagined there could be such overflow, maintenance, and production abroad in the world. Such planning seemed impossible. Who stacked all this? By what means? Beyond strong backs, all she knew was the immediate management of wood. The ox teams must be as mythical as their driver. Beyond the pane, an agile and swift swing arm selected and then dropped parts into a hopper with a compromised bottom. She watched perfect widgets whirl away down a black shaft. As she watched the contraption tipped out nothing onto a feeder rail which had once been longer but now began and ended on the same slab.

"Out there," said Ilea Lark Urkl, "There is no waste. For we dig for fire. For the flame of the breath." The crone, entering, spoke with such cryptic weight even a farm girl found her pronouncements overburdened. The berth admitted a last breeze from the corridor before it closed. "Knock, knock," said the crone. She was now attired as the others. A more supple fur graced her collar, a different sheen glided up her sleeves, which were decorated by different charms. Her doughy hag's face floated into the pane first, pleated and worldly, loose like the farrier's mitt, a terrible ghost haunting the savage landscape. The girl did not look away from the passing scenery. "The interstices certainly impress," said the crone, "Once you see them as such." She drew the curtain wider. "Though I suppose that explains nothing to you. You should not feel alone. Few ever see these spaces. Or even imagine they exist. For them, the city has never changed. Or else degrades. Either way the illusion is expensive to maintain." The crone's features were old but not sexless—there was surely a woman drowned within—but there was also something goatish beyond either gender, an unearned mechanical certitude living in the eyes. "You are to take your place in the songs of angry men." This last the crone sang as a creaky lullaby, hoping to draw away or animate the girl's dull stare. The girl wondered if everyone was going to speak to her in this way, in long passages about objects beyond the partitions of the berth, about things beyond her reach or comprehension. This did not seem real or legal. She was hungry.

"I do not need anything," insisted the girl with a stridency she could not suppress. She now suspected the preceptors could invade her thoughts at any moment and wondered what she could do to obscure her own mind.

She imagined her life on the terraces over-looking the carriageway, the brutal lines under a gray sky, the industrial scale. They were vacant. In her dream life, she decided she would be the only one allowed to venture outside.

"I see we've a long way to go," said Ilea Lark Urkl. "Draw up your blanket if you are cold. Try to leave your wound alone. Together, we are to spend days between stations." The articulated shifted down to descend a sudden change of grade with a terrible and surprising crash. Elektra stifled her surprise. The crone clutched at the divan.

"Would you care for me to fill your cup. You look thirsty. Shall I send for Skiboo?" The girl felt herself rise slightly in the cushions.

"I do not live in delicacies," said the girl too deliberately, provoking a guffaw from the crone.

"Nevertheless," she said, "We should really do something about your hair." Ilea Lark Urkl continued with something that could not filter through the turbine whine. The crone's words could not overcome the resonance of the tunnel through which the articulated now howled. To the girl the sound was like being inside the noise the bucket made against the sides of the well when drawn up empty.

"Have you been able to pry her away?" asked Jon Hauk Or.

"Little steps," creaked Ilea Lark Urkl.

A pressure wave threw a warp through the porthole glass, the world therein becoming deranged, disproportioned. Dank air seeped in around the gaskets as they relaxed.

They had come through the tunnel.

"Why haven't you sent for bandages?" asked Jon Hauk Or.

"She has frequent thoughts of escapes," said the crone, who batted about for her bag of embroidery. "Flights of fancy. She bears watching."

The girl, still faithful to her post, resolved hers would be the fiercest focus on the immediate, come what may. Her world would be the one before her face, within easy reach of her hooks. She would set nothing akindle by accident or otherwise. Elektra did not quit the recamier. She refashioned her face into its most incurious mask. The feel of making it was exactly like adopting the look that made her mother coo and caress her hair; it was also the look that overcame her before she wept.

"Are you sure you don't just want to watch her bleed?" said the man, raising his voice, "Perverse old woman."

"I want to determine how far she will pursue this logic of harm," said the crone, drawing herself up from the divan. Jon Hauk Or made an expansive gesture toward the door, upon which it opened. In the black mirror that was the girl's world, the distorted wraith of Ilea Lark Urkl slipped from the berth, ceased to harrow the land. When the girl looked back,

Jon Hauk Or had adopted her spot. The laws on his sleeves shimmered up his arms in the light cast from the mesh.

That night or the next the articulated stopped to acquire another carriage. They stood by, off clock and schedule, in a wide expanse of a switch yard, the integrated gold of the carriageway glimmering beneath grade. There was a descending thrum although they could not see the street. The vacant terraces above caught the light at the natural hours, the cooperatives above glowed with meshlight of every color until flickered away in a prismatic spray. She saw silhouettes appear briefly and wondered if she looked any different when being looked at herself by someone outside. They waited a day, going by their own mesh's bells, in the doldrums of such thoughts.

Jon Hauk Or came and went, and occasionally snoozed with his legs out in a sunbeam. In the dark there echoed the occasional distant copulation of the articulated being recomposed. The shock came minutes after the boom. She did not like this little jolt or the monotone light which made all the freight moving by orange.

From her dim berth, she watched infiltrators at large in the yard. They shuffled past their carriage, a chorus of men in torn shirts who squared up to one another a stone's throw from the glass. They did not fear the darkened vehicle nor the observers within. They were intent only upon each other. Elektra watched across a passing flatbed. She could not be certain but the most massive of them had a dark knob just above his eyes which his ragged headgear could not completely conceal. The product of a terrible wounding incompletely healed or perhaps a vestigial horn under a humped and stained turban. She cannot be certain because she has never seen or heard tell of a joggle. She has never even heard the tales of the horned men. She cannot know they are the same.

"What are they going to do?" asked the girl.

"Our ghost speaks," said Jon Hauk Or. She had forgotten him and turned, startled. The preceptor smiled at the girl.

"They are joggles," said Jon Hauk Or, "And joggles always do what joggles do."

"Are they are going to hurt each other?" asked the girl.

"Oh yes." The preceptor paused, considering. "But I doubt it will be memorable."

To either flank of their massive leader, the shadows ran a gamut of sizes and semi-crippled postures. Those who stood higher than her knee were contorted as if from chemical incompetence. These stumbled by arcs in broken shoes, released from any directive control now that their leader stood his ground.

The turbaned joggle smiled pleasantly in the orange light, spat into his hand, and stepped forward to shake as if to seal the peace. His mark, a sack-gutted man with a profound narcotic stoop, slid to the grip. The joggle with speed belied by his size then slapped a long incision down his opponent's face. His hairy scalp split away and his face was now separated in a weeping diagonal above the nose, running forehead to jowl. For a moment the revealed bone and teeth shone bright. Elektra, shocked, turned away from the wail and the scuffle.

"You see, ghost, they conceal blades in their cheeks," explained Jon Hauk Or gently, touching his own fine lips. The preceptor became absorbed and visibly amused by his own explanation. "Sometimes it is just a tooth they sacrifice and keep sharp. Grim business. Joggle life."

"Are they animals?" sobbed the girl. She was tempted to turn back to the sight but the mockery and distress overcame her. "One has a horn," she whispered.

"They laugh when they hurt you," said Jon Hauk Or, "But how they howl should you ever hurt them. You would think the end of the whole world was near." The preceptor lay a long blade, naked, across his knees. Outside a great and urgent scurrying arose. Glass popped. A wayward missile thudded into the hull farther up on the articulated.

"Are we safe?" she asked, "Should we best be moving?"

"This is not the interstices," said Jon Hauk Or leisurely, with a yawn. "This is the city." He stood and leaned to the porthole, the blade in his off hand pivoting the point into the carpet. "Oh my." Elektra first though he had meant to excuse himself of this inattention but then realized he had taken in some new horror.

The earlier victim was now blinded by his own blood, was now less distressed than enraged, yet wholly unequal to navigating the debris left out on the switch yard slab. Given over to fury or his own imminent death, he let his face fall, held out his fists and searched for his horned attacker. The latter, his turban now awry, the root of his horn raw to the world, stepped aside and swatted his hand across the fat man's neck.

"Perhaps we should draw the shade for what follows," said the preceptor. But the girl held fast to the curtains for support and continued to attend. The victim fell across the carriageway relays, in an instant shorn of all emotion. Jon Hauk Or fumbled at the mesh. What had been a man, however degenerate, diminished into something discarded under Elektra's gaze. The gasket popped, hissed, and shut out all sound then the pane grew opaque.

"What," she said sharply, "Does the law have to say about animals?"

"You should see their women," chuckled Jon Hauk Or. "Spectacular." He coupled the syllables together as if slowly composing carriages. The night was canceled in the brief thunderclap of a solenoid on some mast high above thudding closed. The orange cast at once disappeared and the lamps switched over. Sometime later Elektra slept without leaving the recamier. She listened as someone walked down the length of the carriage roof. Whenever she started awake, she found Jon Hauk Or remained on watch.

They were in sunlight again. Such speed had they gathered that any detail of the near world was impossible to register. Jon Hauk Or had left. Elektra was alone. She looked off to the distance and gathered what she could before the middle distance, too, became diluted in momentum. The broken doors of row houses where no one may enter. They had been good once, she thought, and well ordered. Some rabid army had smashed all the individuality out of the once handsome mansard houses. Then there were many rows of low dormitories. Before one wheeled a large brawl among teams of shorn proles and half-clothed wards. Elektra watched them throw shoes at each other. Then there was a grand old hotel standing alone, the city withdrawn around it, isolated from circulation, forgotten by the planner, abandoned in an accidental island of untended greenery. The girl sat alone, innocent of any explanation or idea, or simple instinct to just activate the shade. So long as new sights came nothing could make her think of the wisps of her father's hair rising in the heat. Nor did she wonder whether he had dug himself underground.

She caught no sign of their thatch nor oaks nor even birds. She stopped looking. She wondered whether Ilea Lark Urkl would come with her one-way bird. The girl picked out many fires sprung from barrels, even some set again in the twice-burned hulks of abandoned K-vehicles, their open trunks roaring out flame, and even springing from wide cracks in empty streets, exposing a whole cavern of live coals. I was exchanged against a shovel, thought Elektra, as she gazed into this deep inferno.

To distract herself from this realization, unconscious that such consideration was the foundation of all law, Elektra invented categories for everything made with the intention of putting distance between citizens. Vehicle barriers festooned with wrecks. Condemned thoroughfares far too wide to cross in a straight sprint. Topologically the same, a wall and therefore classed together, whether or not alive with packs of dogs or erratic motorcycles. An embattled prefecture emitted a defensive glare which outdid the failing day and kept back a roiling crowd. The prison they passed, somber and solid, and so near to the carriageway she expected to see faces. All of it gone soon and thankfully so. Elektra packed in new sights. The distant towers, truly massive she realized, remained steady while those in the middle ground passed from view with the stateliness of clouds, their upper stories lost in sunset banks of vermilion and teal pollution.

"Drinks are served," announced Jon Hauk Or from the companionway, "Crema. Korova. I'll conduct you to the saloon. Skiboo. Hot drinks just downstairs." When Elektra could turn no further to the porthole Jon Hauk Or leaned across and tapped at the glass and all it contained.

"Be reassured. We are for other, more clement precincts. He wore his fur-trimmed robe. "Don't fret," he said, "You can forget all this. Everything is slated for deblayment."

Elektra did not fret or much move or wonder what deblayment meant. Such was her faith that more would be revealed by adopting an even greater degree of immobility. She turned but did not speak. She drove her thumb into her wrist. Laws she could not read threaded gleaming spirals against each other up either sleeve of Jon Hauk Or. They joined in silver thread at common words. The preceptor shot his cuffs and held his arms stiffly in the hope that she might begin. He put his palms to the glass, let the constricted tempo of the articulated's speed charge his arm. This girl must be given every opportunity, he thought. Had he not already given her the first words. *We are the flame of the breath.* But she had again grown dull of affect.

"Why not come down to the saloon," said Jon Hauk Or, with hearty and insistent warmth.

His tone grew intimate. "We are preceptors, it is true. But you are to be charged to still others. We are only the old. Full of ourselves. No longer reliable as educators. We have learned all the lessons and we know each others' stories. The best of us still have a fair measure of music. The rest at least still hum the words."

"What are you to me, now?" the girl dared ask. She closed her mouth quickly lest a spark escape.

"Now we do errands. Messages and rescues. Like you. Technical exchange. The others call us 'birds' behind our backs. It grows late. Come play cards. I will teach you canasta." The articulated progressed in a constant whisper of a bolt of cloth being separated against a blade.

"What is your name, anyway?" he asked unguardedly, growing bored. Jon Hauk Or waited for her to speak, a tender patience plain upon his long features. "We will not remake you to simply observe," he said, "Or, for that matter, just to play canasta. Come away."

And still the girl did not surrender her name. Nor did she begin to read. She turned away from the laws. She remained seated, pressed herself to the wall until she felt her bones creak. No matter. The girl watched the towers jump out into new relief against gathering clouds, their long faces traced in green light. Enormous spired residences reworked her sense of scale once she was near enough to make out the bays. Dominion blocks connected by causeways and cantilevers. A high straight line of airships rode a meridian. A concentration city, the size of a mountain, massive yet intimate, in spite of its distance. There must be a girl there, she thought, looking out who sees me in this light. Jon Hauk Or grimaced. His mustache was thick with splenda.

"Come away," he said. "Sweet hot Skiboo. Come down to the saloon. Come whenever. Wear your shoes. Or whatever." But Elektra, still dull before the porthole, fell asleep, her ears just tickled by the rasp and twang of a banjo and the hearty refrains of common song.

The towers were gone when she woke. She must be among them now, Elektra realized, passing at their bases, everything but fluted pilasters lost to haze and proximate perspectives. The near city was a low terracotta blur. She wondered whether the articulated's passage caused great clamor in the apartment blocks. Did their echo chase down the promenades, break against rubble? Did it rattle the public meshes at every street corner, the shuttered houses, the people hiding within.

A nail house stood out proudly alone on its pedestal of earth. It was surrounded by a canyon of tower bases with wide corner bays. The construction pit made a moat of rainwater, active pumps, and idle earth movers. She had seen such places here and there protected from destruction by some administrative magic trick. In this case there was also man standing at the bridge with a long black blade cradled in his arms. Where one law ends, another takes root, thought Elektra. Half in a dream she put herself at the foot of steps which led up from the pit and then sent her mind up, scampering at first as if called to supper, then taking the stairs two at a time as if she carried news only she could tell, then winded and slowly as if burdened by a lie, finally with an occasional backward step, as if she were approaching the wrong address. But in her dream it was impossible that the humble gables of the nail house be any other than hers. She could not escape. She could not get used to the pit. She wondered how she would evade the sentinel's blade once she was too clapped out to duck. Would the sentinel bury her body in a nail grave, a tower of earth set aside to bury the dead? Or would the sentinel just tip out her bones to the excavators?

Then Ilea Lark Urkl entered the berth, already stooped to an imposture of excuse, appearing injured before a referee, or as if she did not want to startle a strange ox. How strangely crabbed the preceptor seemed. How muddled was the girl from whom forgivenesses had never once been solicited. Elektra gathered her blanket. Her feet found her clogs. She made to move, abandon the berth. When the ancient preceptor squatted to sit on the banquette beside the mesh, her whole body seemed to search for support in every direction at once, like a calf struggling to stand but in reverse. When she finally settled into stability, her farrier's mitt of a face unwound with the most elaborate relaxation.

"I see you are still stuck," creaked Ilea Lark Urkl, "Mired in observation." The woman hacked out a noxious laugh that hung in the air. "Do you miss your lakes? I would." Who was this preceptor affecting the airs of a girl? Elektra wonders, "What lakes?" but makes no reply. Ilea Lark Urkl produced an embroidery hoop, screwed a monocle into her eye, began the stitch which took her away from the girl with blood streaked on her trousers.

"Suppose we stopped," said the girl. "Suppose we stopped and suppose I gave you my arm and we hobbled on down there." She indicated the promenades which made her a liar by promptly rising above the articulated as the carriageway changed grade. They crossed through the shadows. When they came out onto a wide plaza, the girl saw no robed figures any longer, no retired eminences, but a riot of woolly heads, colorful shirts, pointed shoes, a vibrant frenzy of slaps, furtive hand-to-hand distribution of many small objects. "Could you pick out for me what is going on? Could we stroll on down there and you explain?"

"There is no understanding to be had," said Ilea Lark Urkl, "I am too old to see that far."

"They are selling one another Bash," said Jon Hauk Or, "A substance which renders them joyous and dreamy, which heals rifts. But the drug's true function is to ensure death before breeding. A single taste insures this." The girl was less surprised by this information than the presence of the second preceptor. He stood in the dark corner opposite the crone, beside the mesh. Elektra had taken him for a portmanteau.

"Touch the porthole," he said, "To draw the view near." Why had he not explained this before? Elektra was intrigued. She would do some exploring.

The articulated went into a bend, slowed. As before, this allowed Elektra to see ahead. The vista did not surprise her less. The prom-enades now spanned the carriageway by cat-walks, suspended bridges, and improvised passerelles. Men here, apparently, could fly through the air. And she believed this until she understood they were, in truth, graceful and composed suicides. Beneath every bridge there was intense activity, not war but not peace. The girl touched the porthole pane with both hands and took in the citizens and hands and wards, boys at large, the women who either invited attention or hid within heavy veils, jog-gles given berth among them, with their massy turbans or gaily-painted horns. Did they do this decoration themselves, wondered the girl, or was it done to them? Do they have wives? Something about the opulence and chaos of this new marketplace made her imagine slaves.

Indeed, a joggle with tusks curling back into the flesh of his cheeks held the lead of a fat woman who gamboled before him. Behind him coursed a wave of spectators which gathered to the balustrades, and overflowed up the stairways to the bridges. From hand to hand went plantains, iron bowls, a blue fruit she could not identify, tools, and cans. The slave woman mounted the balustrade, arranged her tether behind her, raised her hands, and plummeted. As the lead ran out the crowd grew excited, breaking into joyful spasms when the joggle released his end of the line, raising his empty hand to the crowd in triumph. In this place, thought Elektra, a broken pact was not only a revel for those one held dear. It was the only way to live.

Elektra caught the eye of an absurd joggle child, pale as the day, with down-turned horns, a tower of unruly hair between them, and the evil aspect of a goat. They had time to take each other in. Dull stare to dull stare but also a slow smile which Elektra chose not mirror. The child grew gloomy. They stared at one another until a squared-off rock, a paving stone she thought later, suddenly obscured his image, overpowering the elasticity of the pane. A cracked ventured out from the gasket and the glass began to squeak apart. Behind her the crone wailed in warning. The goat-child's features began to distort. Elektra first lost his eyes, then his reedy body, his waving hands, his horns, the now exasperated and joyful eyes, everything but the leer but the smile. His bespoke satisfaction dispersed as his teeth flashed apart in a panache of orange sparks. She was to see it again and again. Will this be me some day soon? Her hand found the sore on her arm. Elektra would never really shake the final image of this little sharpshooter. She would conjecture, in memory, that maybe he had wanted to converse.

But first the real rain began.

The initial stone had been a signal. The promenades cut loose. Shaped bricks, keystones, all sorts of ornaments. The initial shower was mostly pavers but stranger objects found their way through the panes. Batteries were flung by the dozens, sent up with elastic catapults. As were bottles filled with urine. Dead animals. From the floor she watched a round white stone rebound, hit the wall above her head, and come to rest where she sheltered under the recamier. A marble cherub's head with full cheeks, smooth, but spalled by ricochet somewhere along its recent flight. This was followed by a black quarrel fletched with ragged feathers. This missile careened across the berth crazily, scoring a groove across the table, before slapping into the companionway beyond. The girl caught the odor of carburant, of cleaning fluid, of blood. Some of all this clatter was presumably the crone. The volley did not cease but grew in force and frequency and now rode a hearty cheer. Elektra did not see what had happened to Ilea Lark Urkl. She heard an alarm, vaguely distant, somewhere farther forward in the vehicle, barely beating the noise. Somewhere else, it was worse.

In the saloon nobody said a word. Elektra sidled in, unnoticed. Oddly, nobody seemed outraged or bitter. Jon Hauk Or arranged the crone on a divan. She had been thumped by a rounded stone directly between the dugs. The train personnel stood by and muttered. This unprovoked attack was just something to be taken in stride. He opened her collar, held her head back, looked into her mouth, put his own lips over her yellow teeth, and blew her back to life. The floor was littered with missiles, packaging, stones, cladding. Paneling swung free from moldings, wood friezes traced in carved animal motifs, horses chasing a fox, all hanging by the finishing nails.

"Not to make excuses," coughed Ilea Lark Urkl upon waking, closing her cloak to hide again the waddle and fleshy fans below her chin, "But the same stuff goes on anywhere." Although she addressed the room, Elektra supposed the comment was meant for her alone. The crone rose from the divan, revealing that the seat-back allowed through daylight where it had been shredded by shrapnel. "It all comes down to playfulness and little pranks." They all murmured assent, even admiration for the crone's long experience of the world, as the articulated regained its speed although the alarm continued to blare.

Will my body one day become like the crone's? wondered Elektra. There must be some substance not Bash.

"Today it was just our turn," said Jon Hauk Or to the room, reasonably. He stood and cleared the colored balls and debris from the billiards table, upon which he spread a map so large it flopped to the floor. The sight of an assistant controller bringing him a small stemmed glass on a tray caused him to brighten even more. He abandoned the map for a moment, rubbed his hands together, accepted the glass. The preceptor swished the aquavit from one cheek to the other, then spat it into the clutter. Elektra took in its energetic smell and thought of her father half gone by the fire.

Jon Hauk Or spoke in the tone which settled the room to a warm murmur. "Sooner or later it happens to everyone." He straightened his hair and went back to marking out a heavy red box upon the sheet.

Besides the preceptors, stewards in pillbox hats and technicians in hard suits, finished with helping each other from the floor, were now milling about, stunned by the damage and the fury. Most were asking what had happened, making dry remarks that would have seemed unfunny to Elektra under other circumstances.

"Could we go around again?" said a porter.

"I didn't quite hear you," said another with a bloody head, "Over the ringing bells."

The girl had not supposed so many crew were necessary to operate the articulated. Aside from the preceptors she had thought herself alone, important, ensconced in a system which ran itself along pre-decided lines, guided by protocol as straight as the meridians along which were drawn the airship caravans, everything managed beyond the reach of fallible hands.

Outside, through unprotected air, she saw the snout houses and their open garages, remarkably like a row of pigs aligned to the long trough of a street, heavily lined with collection. She saw the moment where each house accepted its own K-vehicle. They proceeded at ordered intervals, staggered down the row, almost exactly in time with the passage of the articulated. The street bleeding off its full congestion. "Exactly upon the conclusion of the congested hour," said a skinny boy wearing the pillbox hat of a steward, "Extraordinary, isn't it?" When he tapped his hat it made a hollow sound.

The crew gathered in the saloon, coming up from more distant regions of the articulated. Many had blood on their clothes and walked leaned to a mate, but upon entering, they caught their superiors' light mood. They grumbled funny remarks as they passed. Some looked at Elektra but not too long. A controller with a gold braid across his chest was pres-

ent with a torch nobody needed and distribut-
ed blandishments to which none responded.
"Little kids!" he said, "Imagine. Glanton, did
you see? Adolescents in their disgusting tribes!
Why I have a little Hottentot myself, waiting at
home station. I suppose it is the same for you
Simkins. Or was it two? Come now Simkins,
how many up and down the line?"

"Joia, Tripod, Manufactory, Chicago
Inferior," said Jon Hauk Or, lost in consideration. He snapped his fingers to draw the controller's attentions to the map, his finger making bright splashes on the paper. "Look here,
man. What's next?" he asked.

"The Swallowtail," answered the controller.

"Divert," said the preceptor, using his hand
to measure scale, wishing he had more time
to find better answers. "Take Salguero. Take
anything. Robert's Cut Off. Shore Ditch Drive."

"We've engaged the Swallowtail, excellency." The controller put his hands behind his
back but bent forward, feigning greater concentration. "I threw the switch just before
coming forward. The toll was assessed and
confirmed just as we were hit."

"No two things happen at the same time,"
muttered Jon Hauk Or, "And there are no co-
incidences." The controller gestured with the
torch he used to guide passengers through
low light. "We're almost through the Straight."
He meant to encourage but his voice sounded
hollow, even thin.

The snout houses receded after a brief series of brownfields where stray dogs trotted down paths grown over with chokeweed and black krop. The towers to either side of the now narrowed carriageway approached steadily, meaning they were near. Elektra went to a porthole in the corridor just outside and did the trick on the pane to enlarge the view. The massive floral appliques across the faces of the towers were blackened with a pox of irregularly set windows. A long beard of rust from exposed fixtures ruined the effect of a delicately graphic chrysanthemum. The articulated was making for the light of the distant lake where the Swallowtail proper began.

"Shall I budget for more speed?" the controller was asking when Elektra re-entered. The man had hoped to appease the preceptor glaring at the map. It was not going well.

"Your name?" asked Jon Hauk Or, "Just for the record."

"Prather, excellency," said the controller.

Jon Hauk Or boxed the Swallowtail in red upon the map. A long curve was there drawn in hachures indicating the carriageway was not level. Probably it had been canted for a previous generation of less advanced conveyance. The preceptor put down the crayon. The zone as delimited did indeed make half a swallow's tail considered in concert with the curve of the lake shore. The girl wondered if the effect was deliberate, the caprice of some junior planner.

Little of what she had seen since leaving her father seemed untouched or left to nature.

"Prather," said Jon Hauk Or, "Thicken the spectrum. Slop up every mesh until they bleed chartreuse. No word travels before us. Nothing passes. Declare an emergency if someone protests." The preceptor's earlier ebullience had dissipated. Prather began to pick his way through the wreckage, trailing a length of chintz which had come away from a sundered vanity partition. On his way he accidentally trod on the preceptor's discarded aperitif glass. It broke with a plink. Prather stopped, and stood holding his foot.

"And Prather?" queried the preceptor without looking away from his plan, "Do please put on more speed." Jon Hauk Or looked up, poised and reasonable. In that moment, the girl came to admire him. Perhaps it was just an effect of the blue-green light. She looked forward to his future attention. I will tell him my true name, she decided, I will risk a spark.

The preceptor pointed at Ilea Lark Urkl, who had by now regained as much of her composure as her rickety posture would allow. "Go forward," said the preceptor, "Find the girl a wagon where the hull still enjoys integrity. Remember, she has no inoculation. I want her out of the wild air and pollen."

Outside, a relay of mirrors suddenly sparkled across the tower tops, like light across water, in rapid sequences of sharp flashes re-layed forward.

They picked their way back, accustomed to each other, the crone clutched to the girl, the girl conducted by the crone down a passage outlined in dim light set into the floor, un-stable yet intent, shuffling to the side togeth-er when the articulated shifted. They moved through the last of the Straights with the free air pouring in all around them, past places where the hull had been rent open by debris. The smell of kerosene and fry oil permeated the companionway. Was life different in these carriages? Elektra wondered.

Elektra heard a whistle from outside, a long note which normalized her ear to its sharp-ness and did not die. The missiles began again where the lake weakly lapped at the carriage-way. They felt a loud bang, a pressurized in-terval, and then a shudder ran down the spine of the articulated as each wagon leaned into the bank. The vehicle canted over distressing-ly, spilling the girl and the crone, and began to rise, sliding into the rise on the force of its momentum. The porthole now gave to the blur of the carriageway.

This time the debris had been prepared, positioned for tipping over in one moment, along the whole line of the articulated. A toilet bowl wheeled down, well timed, put to free-fall at the perfect moment, almost noble along its trajectory, in perfect synchronicity with the articulated's approach to the outside observer, until it met the vehicle's most forward compartment. All manner of fittings and objects followed, already airborne. Dishwashers, bed frames, chairs of every form, shopping carts laden with pavers, shopping carts with their contents aflame, an antique hall clock, fans of copy, lamps fashioned of wire and unbleached paper, single light bulbs, toy animals with limbs spread rigidly to receive embrace, souvenir scrolls, ornamental swords, a sleeve of lacquered nesting tables which expanded into a delicate arc as it fell, retaining an internal sense of order, model airships decorated with crooked decals of defunct empires, breviaries, and all manner of other books. It all came down upon the articulated with varied effect. A spray of colorful sporting equipment separated in a scatter. Now it came from both sides of the carriageway as if a team hidden from view was executing a secret play. The hoarded contents of entire lives thundered down until there was nothing left to throw. Food stuffs, cash, servitors still blinking with incomprehension, a matte murderball trophy as black a bit of space, a sheet of liquid aflame.

The articulated freed itself from the bend and was threading its way through a gap beneath an aluminum tower when it ground to a stop, at that moment receiving whatever could be torn from the tower itself. Indeterminate

hunks of finishing, plaster and polished con-
crete, dismantled plumbing, a heat exchanger,
radiators, armored doors, an obsolete mesh its
capacitors still holding sufficient charge that its
face flickered with a traditional laff riot, briefly bearing the image of a man entrained into
a gear, working furiously with his wrenches,
although certain to be ground apart.

Then came the animals. The first and last
flight of live animals bred under meshlight
were unceremoniously uncrated to clear skies.
Flailing squalling pinwheels of cats, an air-pad-
dling retriever—their instinctive flailings did
nothing to change or arrest their terminal tra-
jectories. Soon the living bodies of the resi-
dents themselves came as a dire surprise, careening end over end with their hands bound
or else held outward in a way which recalled
the stuffed toys. These unfortunates came
seeded into their furniture and houseplants
like an afterthought. They splashed into the
wagon hulls, some bouncing away, broken, a
short distance, all ending in a distressing and
bloody disassociation. Elektra and the crone
sheltered in a closet and watched through the
sundered door.

Then came the dead, as sometimes happened even on days when no articulated passed
through the Swallowtail. They came wrapped
in sheets or simply naked. And then came the
old, wheeled away from sunny nooks familiar to them, their oxygen masks re-affixed, be-

fore being introduced to the air. Next to the growing dump came grimly composed adults, dressed for afternoon business, silent in shiny shoes, hands to their robes to keep their lower bodies from coming unclothed, dignified and resigned, not seeking the earth at all. By now nothing ended in a thud against the hull of the articulated. Nothing now crashed apart on the carriageway, except those pieces which had already crashed apart against other detritus. The vehicle had been stopped cold at its head by the initial toilet and it lay exhausted of movement like a noble bird on the forest floor, still sprawled for flight but struck to earth.

There came a pause, but still the infamy had not ended. By then the crone had rallied Elektra by sinking a claw unto the sore on her arm. Together they had risen and scrambled very far back in the articulated, well beyond its damaged length. Ilea Lark Urkl led the girl into a wide dormitory.

Outside, low figures were beginning to emerge from the lobbies and mezzanines at the tower bases, the grotto-like corner shops, coming together in ragged groups, organizing with the aid of buzzers which made the girl remember the sudden summer arrival of grasshoppers. Already the more daring skels and clockers and lords ventured into the open expanse of the carriageway, their less courageous followers slowly drawing together in a lazy beater's line just to their rear. Those in the

advancing crowd took note of their own number and scale, the parabola of them setting up,
increasing through the space between the corners formed where the carriageway cut across
the square. Satisfied with its size, the crowd
took on a sort of permanency and advanced.
Those in front looked fearfully at the sun, hesitating before deciding the direct light was no
danger. There rose a cheer and a clatter.

The crone activated the shades to make it
all disappear. And so the crone and her charge
missed the moment the defenestration crews
appeared at the limit of their various precipic-
es. Panting from effort, surveying their damage with fevered eyes and wide smiles, they
linked sweaty hands along the rails and balconies, for all the world like a deafened cast
at curtain call before a house maddened with
applause. Attired in the sky blue of their window cult, arm-in-arm they took one step forward and pulled each other out into an otherwise ordinary afternoon. The girl had only
heard them count down, cheerily, giddy. "What
is going to happen now?" she asked the crone,
slightly hysterical herself. Ilea Lark Urkl, cow-
ering, had a suspicion that she did not share.
Better the girl remain innocent of such sinister
organization for a while longer. They sheltered
beneath an infant's changing table and joined
the cultists in counting aloud. The cultists of
all ages held together in trios and quartets, almost all of them straining to contain the one

who could not help but thrash. A pair, neither male nor female yet something thin and sisterly about them, held hands, executed a synchronized pike, meeting the macadam where the carriageway properly began with far less grace than one would expect. An observer of such flawless form would have hoped for something more. But merit did not carry that day.

The buzzing was growing near. The crone unbent herself from the floor with sighs and groans. "Who are the people who do this?" asked the girl who ceased gasping only to break into tears, "Why?" She had only ever seen a tower a day ago. It had seemed so wonderful. She had just begun to project herself into the warmth of life within, a view of the far horizon, easy transport, neighbors all around. Why had her father sought his future underground when a tower was such an obvious solution?

"Try," said Ilea Lark Urkl, drawing a deep breath, "To avoid them in your conscience." The crone peeked through the blinds worriedly. "They will be a moment still," she said quickly, "There is nobody to encourage them. The footing has grown slick. Now they have stopped." The crone sighed in relief.

"When I was your age I rode a mechanical bicycle," said Ilea Lark Urkl, running her claws through Elektra's hair, relaxing the snarls at a touch. The buzzing of the crowd had become rhythmic, had lost the sense of any signal beyond a simple announcement of the crowd's constant presence. "My ride to school toke me through a busy roundabout," continued the crone. "In the midst of the roundabout there was a cast likeness of the last usurper, Thura. I do not remember how avenues met at that junction. I remember a great clatter of bicycles, the lateness of the hour. I remember I could not go wrong if I pedaled up the way Thura favored with his glance. Ah, we once had such statues! This version of Thura no longer stands. My orientation of long ago is lost. Without such likenesses the cults grow worse. Not everyone joins. They manufacture as much meaning as they can by rude insistence. And there are always many more followers than one would expect when the great day is announced. This which we are living through? It will not end today. All orientation was lost long ago. The old way exists, but is deliberately obscured. We have no common song. And there is no more school. Not as I knew it." As if on cue the buzzers took on the cadence of a trot. "It began," said the crone, drawing Elektra's head to her breastbone, "Long before you were born.

"Is this normal city life?" asked the girl.

"You need never go out," said the crone. "Everything is delivered to your door."

The buzzing ceased, nearer. The girl began to whimper. "Do not let them sour you so early in your day," said Ilea Lark Urkl, "Do not look them in the eye." The girl's dominant hand rose to her wrist, attacked. "Let us speak of sisterly things. The lakes of your district. Or tell me of your mother."

The girl could recall no lake, no light on the water, nothing like what she had seen coming around the Swallowtail. There had been a spot on the horizon over which hovered a cloud. Was that the lake? Had her mother left her alone, gone in solo search of water? What other element could have drawn her away from the hearth? Her thumb moved more freely in the blood it drew, enough to make a sloppy sound. The brief sight of the lake at the confluence of the shoreline and the carriageway, just moments ago, the artificial islands, the moored pleasure craft, the grim reservoir intakes drawing water like a vortex to another universe, had stirred nothing in her. What did the crone mean to suggest by insisting upon a lake? She watched Ilea Lark Urkl leaning to the porthole, putting out both arms, either from interest or decrepitude, as if her skeleton could withstand only a little more of either. "Thura be my guide," she said in awed resignation. She opened the shade. The crowd was well formed now and closer than the girl had imagined. Jon Hauk Or strode into the nursery. He went directly to the mesh and passed his hand across its face. It had been tuned to calming pastels. Upon his gesture the mesh took on a deep crimson. He arranged his robes and waited.

"Where are you?" said a voice speaking from the mesh.

"We got as far as the Swallowtail," said Jon Hauk Or.

"What is your order?" said the voice on the other side. The speaker sounded remote and amused, the voice of a demon comfortably seated at the bottom of a well.

"Deblayment," said Jon Hauk Or absently, speaking to himself. The preceptor, hearing his own indecision, brightened with certainty. He spoke more directly to the mesh now, sharply articulating. "Deblayment."

"Release a skutter, perhaps?" asked the voice whimsically. "Have a peek?

Jon Hauk Or's jaw grew firm and his vowels shortened. He was now speaking in spite of himself. "Release a skutter, sure. Immediate disarticulation and retrograde. Shunt to Robert's Cut Off or Salguero. Re-engagement toward least impedance. Consider Shore Ditch if necessary. Maybe the Pits. The skutter will tell." He paused. "Subsequent deblayment upon current position." Perhaps he had been too hasty. "Per local request," he added. His orders received, the crimson was replaced by swirls of blue and yellow. "Well," said Jon Hauk Or, taking in his surroundings, "That's that. Everything is blue and gold." The crowd outside began a jog, roared, and charged. Jon Hauk Or looked up disinterestedly and helped Elektra from the floor.

The girl was confused by the shift of the articulated's detachment. There was a click and a lurch and the square immediately became smaller. The crowd in full charge broke over the remains of the articulated but drew up after a shake and a thud resounded through the lively tail of a worm they had considered slain. Then the girl's body grew light. She felt returned to speed immediately and just as quickly she relaxed to the now familiar sensation. She now sat backwards to their direction of travel. Safety flowed from speed as well as a small measure of joy. Ilea Lark Urkl tottered about the nursery, straightening.

"Say what you will, but even the likeness of an enemy supposes artistry and organization," said Ilea Lark Urkl. She stood up the plushes and stoppered the basins. "This is what happens to a city too long without a statue."

"Where are the children?" asked the girl, "What's kept behind there?" The girl indicated a hatchway encumbered with a pressure seal. It could not lead into another wagon, she surmised, but was a sub-compartment of the current one.

"There are always those who object to transport," said Ilea Lark Urkl, "Not everyone goes along so well as you have. Or comes so far."

"'Rescue' is the modern term," said Jon Hauk Or, his legs crossed, sitting at a kitchen island. He was absorbed in watching overhead feed from the skutter on a tiny screen. "Kindly

172

excuse your minder." He crossed to a settee and lay down.

The crone ignored him. She walked around his boots and folded cots down from the partitions. "Not so well appointed but sufficient." She was clearing space, and the nursery began to seem larger. They were now careening around a curtain wall, departing from the lake. "Salguero," said Ilea Lark Urkl, presenting the girl with another blanket, exactly the odor of the first. "The given name of The Exile. A sort of pass phrase, I guess. Or the other one. The Cut Off. Ulroc. I'm beyond keeping them straight. Everyone sees me coming, anyway." She patted the blanket in the girl's lap, "Just an old woman. Barely fit for purpose. They'll find me muttering their shibboleths in a gated park, shuffling about in my slippers." Jon Hauk Or yawned in the fading sunlight. "Although I did not hear our new destination spoken," said Ilea Lark Urkl. The tall preceptor lay down, put his arm over his face, and did not answer.

That evening, the girl slept on a fold-out cot over which her legs dangled. She was discomforted by the articulated's every lurch. Yet no further calamity rained down. It felt odd to sleep steps away from where Jon Hauk Or slumbered. She woke at every change in the ramjet's pitch, after every small movement in the near air. After Ilea Lark Urkl woke her picking her way to the exit, the worry that the articulated would again separate from itself without her

noticing crept into her thoughts. Elektra lay
with her eyes closed, newly resolved to notice
everything, to remain awake, to always have
a plan ready. She considered all she had been
through since she had lost sight of her father's
homeward turn. Everyplace seemed an exten-
sion of the fire which claimed the cob house.
Her only idea, should the worst come to pass,
should she be shaken awake and jettisoned,
was to draw the blanket around herself like a
preceptor's cape, run through flames, go headlong toward any open space which did not
burn, climb as soon as she could, get closed
in, hold her breath, disappear. No wonder,
thought Elektra, we spread fire everywhere we
pass. She thought of the black quarrel passing
through the shattered porthole that morning,
spending itself without effect. There had to be
someone behind it, with a windlass and bow,
a stiff spring, a squinted eye. No matter what
speed the articulated attained, the girl felt pursued by that intention. She was certain that
eye was still present. The city was also an oily
blackness as dark as any mirror, a following
lidless eye. It would have been better to draw
the curtain over the porthole, she thought.

They spent a day in a switch yard so much
like the first that Elektra screwed her fists into
her eye sockets hoping to clear the dream. She
looked about for traces of the former combatants, lurching lame survivors. The diminished

articulated remained unremarked save for the faces of the children appearing at the windows of the towers overlooking the yard. At mid-day a truly ancient looking conveyance thundered through to a slow stop. No modern articulated, the ensemble was held together with iron hooks and rotted cables. Oil leaked from the absorbers. The blinds were down in all the short wagons and the plating bore bright scars and glowing burns. Rags of vegetation hung along its length, as if stripped away while making a forced passage on a disused jungle track. Technicians in hazard suits arrived on a squat tender buzzing with power as Elektra watched. They gathered for a short conference, organized their tools on a tarpaulin laid out on the ground.

Elektra ate rice dashed with blackstrap and watched them work without pause on a gantry, hoisting out and changing the core in the lead wagon. A chain clicked through the hoist twice and doubled its magic powers. The yard caught the pale green pallor of the nearly-exhausted pile. This was, thought Elektra, the sight meant to distract her. So she put down her rice and looked elsewhere, running her eye along the length of the vehicle's vines and jury-rigged barding and so caught a dark figure when it detached and trotted away under the glare. Its presence excited hounds within earshot but she herself did not rise to the baying. She did not seek to spot the animals scrabbling through the ballast. She drew the curtain.

"Penals," observed Ilea Lark Urkl with tight-jawed judgment, "Thieves. Slaves on a midnight frolic. Organizing an escape." She bit into a slice of lemon, placing the rind on the saucer. "Be assured. Down the line punishment awaits."

"I didn't wonder," said the girl.

"Ah," exclaimed the preceptor, "I did not mean to unsettle you. Finish your supper. I will sit with you until you sleep," said the crone, now at her embroidery.

What have I stolen? wondered Elektra, drifting to sleep. What is to be extracted from me? When she woke, the girl found her dreams had changed nothing. There was no warm cow. There was no sleeping father. There had been no fire. No hound at her feet. Her brother had not prepared a draught. Escape had been successful but now that was over.

"There you are," said a restored Jon Hauk Or. The crone was gone save for her faint odor. Naphthalene. "Where did you expect me to be?" said the girl. The preceptor wore a new stars and charms on his sleeve.

"Still glued to your porthole," he said, "So." He shot his cuffs, exposing further law. "What prospect?"

Elektra took this as permission to stretch and look out on the terraces of Salguero in the early sun. The night train had moved on.

She saw green balconies decorated with bottle glass, the blind walls faced with sprays of dying vines, beyond the reach of any good-hearted resident with a watering can. The night train had gone on. She thought of her father trying to scratch his back after a bath. Their house had once been very warm. Then she watched an airship, floating slowly, crosswise to their travel. THERE IS NO ENEMY crawled across its envelope, the letters running a saturated gamut from red to violet as each word dissolved into the next.

Elektra remembered she had been asked a question. She snorted at her answer before blurting "There is no enemy."

"Quite," said Jon Hauk Or, bowing slightly and looking skyward.

"We are not so far from the varsity now," said Jon Hauk Or, "Your new life is meant to begin there. But there is yet a little more to take in."

She felt a slight chill across her skin. As if her mother had drawn the twice-used towel across her back.

The sky held more light where they were. Jon Hauk Or glared up into the clouds. "A massive statuary will come into view any moment now. Or, rather, its remains." He retreated to the mesh. "It has been under constant assault for years. Something of a spectacle. Let's have a look." He worked a dial at the mesh. "Show me the first one to fall," he said into the grill.

The articulated sighed into a long curve and braked. They passed a massive excavation, a cascade of stairs carved into the walls, people wrapped in oatmeal-colored cloth hauling jerry cans up from a chartreuse pool. Any slip would seem to be fatal. The risers were faced in bright blue and green ceramic. Elektra wondered whether she would ever pass this way again, whether she would have the courage to descend such a stair. Oatmeal people rested on the landings, met with their counterparts coming up, stood aside as best they could. They bent beneath the poles upon which they hung their cans. The stairs were slick with spillage, thick with neighbors. At the level of the pool, which Elektra could only see by standing in her seat, children disappeared beneath the duckweed, surfacing after long intervals. Was this labor performed every day? she wondered and grew worried.

"What is a statuary?" asked the girl.

"A statuary," said Jon Hauk Or, "is the image of a man wrought in metal or stone." The preceptor waved away a spray of numerals emanating from the mesh and then conjured a warrior on a horse which soon outgrew his palm, filling the space beyond the mesh until it intruded upon the girl, who pulled her arms to her sides and shrank away. "The one we're coming onto was a real colossus. Note the animal upon which he is seated. This is an idealized horse. Perhaps you've heard stories of them. Slightly less terrible to behold in flesh and bone."

Elektra decided to admit no such ignorance of horses. The idea of such public art gave her pause. "What does that mean?" she asked. "What do you mean it is under assault?"

"It means," he said, "That artistry was once done on a scale at least as grand as the resentment with which it is now met. These days, the best the city can do is rude idols." The preceptor waved away the statuary and summoned to the fore an autonomous freighter pitching in heavy seas, clone sheep at play on its decks, a bright animated countdown which taught numerals in a language composed of clicks and coughs. There was ever another image to be had from the mesh. The girl thought that one day she would try to exhaust the device, just paw and gesture at it until it could no longer advance beyond some final scene or scandal. The girl thought that maybe she would rather carry up cans of chartreuse on an unsure stair.

The preceptor settled upon a wide image of a crowd overcoming barricades by climbing up each other's backs then flowing into a wide, white space, their dark mass negatively delimiting walls and arcades which continued into the foreground of the shot, implying the possibility of safe remove.

"Insects," croaked Ilea Lark Urkl, "In spite of their attire. They're all wired the same upstairs."

"This is still yesterday for me," said Jon Hauk Or absently, his fingers at play within the image as if searching for an individual phantom to pluck out for inspection. "I was just about here," he said, putting his finger through a public fountain. Elektra recognized a tiny figure with the preceptor's stately gait. It stopped and put its foot up on the bench around the basin. The sprite's upright posture kept it from assimilated into the throng.

Then the focus reversed to show the crowd closing around a pedestal the size of a cathedral, the size of the perimeter around the chartreuse pit. Where the footing was uncertain, the crowd wavered and fought against itself. A pushing and pulling ensued, which made the girl think of her father shoveling dirt through a sieve. The weak set to scrapping in the wake of the real force pushing forward. In the near distance towers burned. On floors below those bright with destruction, witnesses gathered upon the terraces. Now the focus pulled forward in a precise and steady swoop, centering on a white hot image. Once the sensors balanced and the image resolved, the girl could make out a man borne on the back of a beast, as when her father placed her atop the ox, but with more poise. It was not a horse, but Elektra held her peace. Perhaps this was therefore not a statuary. Seen from overhead again, the insects overcame their reluctance, swarming through the shadow of the colossus, pushed up the stairs, and crashed to the pedestal. From yet another graceful and precise angle, the girl saw the beast better, profiled against a rising cloud of gas. She decided the animal is from the storybook, the chapter about the elk or stag. Although its ears and face are wrong. After a moment's further consideration, she understood the beast's elegant ears were not horns.

"The cavalier was also a preceptor, you know," said Jon Hauk Or wistfully, "in later life." Then he spoke in the tone of voice he reserved for setting an instruction. "You are looking at the Necessary Cavalier. We are a continuation of his line."

Together they watched the images of the mesh, a whole panoply of wild and swift overhand swings, a war of all versus all, blows delivered with little art and much shouting. Ghostly combat filled the nursery. The girl watched the scrum. Joggled-up youths with their locks knotted and spiked for war were bowled over by their own overcommitment to dealing haymaker harm.

The shot now ran down a thin, google-eyed line of a welfare committee in gas capes, their faces erased by black protective rubber. They briefly held rank. They retreated with arms linked, their menacing air overcome by the mass, but otherwise intact. Now the Necessary Cavalier remained stoic in the frame, his hat resembling a sail from this angle, his chin and outstretched arm raised high over the smoky trajectory of the welfares' grenades. Joggles rolled about on the pavement and were struck. There were no parries, no feints, no art to their fight, just a fury of pure energy, a continued machinelike pulse of blood and scuffle. K-cycles and scooters lay abandoned, some with their throttles stuck and the wheels still spinning; joggles fell as their pantaloons aspirated into the chains and drives. They cried out and set each other's teeth to the curb and kicked. Tightly turbaned hair, frazzled hair, braids, blinking cycle helmets took most of the heat of the blows made to their heads. Only dazzlers and hazing agent gave them any pause. "He wore the same laws on his sleeves," said Jon Hauk Or, "No matter how times I watch this assault, the thought never leaves me."

"It bears no incidence," wailed Ilea Lark Urkl sourly from somewhere within the hologram, "Beyond that which we lend."

Elektra could no longer see into the step well beyond the porthole. A sullen crowd congregated at street level, ignoring the food vendors, waiting for a turn to descend. Within the nursery, the mesh tableau set out by Jon Hauk Or of the recent past continued to boil with tiny figures in torn clothes. Cat People clawed their way over the bloodied Island Boys with yellow hair and even overcame the Owl Tribe, pulling away their ostentatious false beaks.

The focus puller selected a portly man with makeup whiskers scrawled over his jowls in beauty pen. False ears had been pressed to his scalp. He had turned at the base of the pedestal as if he had won the right to speak. He removed his shirt as if this were proper, revealing a fine coat beneath. Jon Hauk Or held his hand over the figure to dispel the crowd noise, so all could hear him squeak. In a child's voice he made his ecstatic announcement.

"Welcome to peace," said the Cat Person.

"So you see, girl," said Ilea Lark Urkl, "What we are up against."

The tableau grew in scale, shrinking away, to show the crowd passing up lengthy hardware, still joggled to each other, but this common labor had some calming effect. Spars and planks were handed overhead. Brawls became knots and knots broke into teams passing up crates of pins and sledges and anchors and cables. Jon Hauk Or pumped his fist through the image and the sun rose and set at speed. Level after level was knocked together, the square occasionally ringing with the accidental chorus of syncopated hammers. The mesh fell silent long before completion as its hourly budget expired.

"No matter. We will see what remains of their works from atop the next rise," said Jon Hauk Or.

"How far did they go?" asked the girl, "What did they want?"

"That day, they dropped the cavalier's arm. With charges, levers, manual saws. The actual process has been suppressed from meshflux."

When they came around into the bright valley ringed by utility parks and, in their center, a broad square. "You are beginning to catch the rhythm?" asked Ilea Lark Urkl, "The heart of every district was meant to be an empty space."

"Ladies," announced Jon Hauk Or, "The Necessary Cavalier." But the amplitude of the preceptor's gesture failed him. First Elektra perceived it as a tree, a savaged canopy split by a storm or an errant vehicle. The tree rose above regularly arranged mid-rises. Her mind struggled with the scale, finally supposing it could be a very far-away tree. Then she could make out the eyes of the beast, which just overlooked the eaves. The cavalier's mount. These shabby buildings had been thrown up since the initial assault. It did not look anything like the image on the mesh. A stag, she thought, like the one she once saw abandoning a winter field.

"They have had the head off," whispered the preceptor, now beside her at the window. "I had not heard." Ilea Lark Urkl rocked back in her seat to create the momentum necessary to rise and join them. She hobbled over holding to the flashing.

❁

"The have had his head off," she repeated, needing to confirm the sight to herself, "And they have rolled it away somewhere."

Jon Hauk Or's voice grew leaden, worried, questioning. "To enter within?"

The stag was indeed burdened with a headless torso in uniform whose remaining arm held a plumed hat. The articulated neared. The carriageway rose. The three of them looked into what remained of the broad square the girl had seen on the mesh. Even at distance, they were dominated by the plinth, whose shadow the articulated crossed. The massive arm lay upon shattered flagstones at the center, its palm open to the sky.

Jon Hauk Or spoke into the mesh.

"Prather? Are you with us still?"

"So I am, sir."

"Prather, please put in a stop." The controller refused, citing an accounting difficulty, insurance clauses, risk procedures, and local geology.

"Put it on the margin," said Jon Hauk Or before he could conclude his complaint, "Send back your torch. And stop, Prather." The preceptor steadied Ilea Lark Urkl at the shoulder and cut off the conductor's further caution mid-sentence. The articulated slowed and the crone held to Jon Hauk Or's restraining hand. As with every massive construction she had seen since leaving home, the girl felt at once near and distant. Feelings of mixed proximities were no longer anything new, she realized, although her mind had to struggle through them, still. Something else disturbed her. Something about the hat. Elektra felt worse, more loomed over, even cold, when they stopped.

Scaffolding erected during the initial assault still stood half tumbled. It had twisted away from the plinth in places but had been re-lashed into service, with a network of monkey bridges strung over crevasses made complex by jutting pipes, pilot cable, and loose chapp. The tallest of these reached to the level of the stag's hooves. At the lowest levels, Elektra could see detritus repurposed to shelters. Tattered blue sheeting blew in the breeze. Tiny wraiths shrouded in that same plastic gathered here and there on the higher protrusions. Elektra put her hands to the porthole, made the scene larger. The base was well beyond an easy climb but the high tide of the crowd's anger had licked the stone with competing slogans and insults layered so densely that Elektra could not tease them apart.

Strange alphabets struggled through each other, none winning free to comprehension, making for a muddy convergence sharing no cognate and painted to the height of one man standing on the shoulders of another. She recognized letterforms that began the basest curses, the echo of interjections she had picked up from the gleaners who stooped dejected in her father's fields on the edge of winter, weeks after harvest, and stopped there exhausted, turning away empty handed.

"All of that paint peels away under its own weight," pronounced Ilea Lark Urkl, "Their signs are always worried away by sleet and thaw and the spalling of the marble beneath. Yes, they ruin surfaces. But the stone beneath is solid. Nonsense comes in festoons!"

The other preceptor looked on, bothered. He diminished the view somehow, in spite of Elektra's contact with the glass. "There lies the arm that was once extended toward a figurative enemy on a far horizon," said Jon Hauk Or. "Warning or promise, he shows the way from which we came and will go. It has lain there since I earned my stripes." He coughed into his elbow and straightened. "Damn it. I fee like a child standing here." And then he quoted the Necessary Cavalier, rapping at the pane. "I could not say the names of their places so I removed them from the map." He laughed. "Now that was quite a statement!"

Ilea Lark Urkl brightened, sensing her opportunity. "A gesture toward a future we can no longer enjoy," she said with transparently insincere grandeur, as if she were overly pleased with an easy trick taken at cards. The cavalier's hand, the girl noted, wore a heavy glove. The braid stood in relief upon the sleeve, still gilded where the limb rose too steeply for an easy scramble. It wound, the girl realized, in the same whirls and coils as did the laws on the preceptor's sleeve.

"See? The scrappers still haven't dared attack the laws," said Jon Hauk Or. He was growing agitated. He belted on his blade, rattled it around his waist to its proper place. "The arm should have been enough. It should have stopped there. I shall descend. I want a look inside."

"Plumb the hollow man for his hollow bones?" suggested Ilea Lark Urkl. But the preceptor was already gone. Just outside their porthole Elektra and Ilea Lark Urkl watched a spirited negotiation between the preceptor and the controller Prather, which ended with the latter pushing back his shako in consternation, and slapping his torch into Jon Hauk Or's palm, and rendering his superior a sarcastic hand salute.

The preceptor's departure had allowed air to enter which burned sweetly and carried a slow sting. What would he find? wondered Elektra. Who would come down to meet him on the carriageway? Fleetingly, the girl fantasized traveling alongside the tall man, adopting something of his stride. Would she have found her brother there in the chilly gloom, unharmed, his arms aloft, ready to be taken up?

Following her fancy, as she watched the preceptor make his way out, she wondered about the head. Suppose it rolled through the city of its own accord, leaving its stern face imprinted on playing fields and in petunia beds. Jon Hauk Or stepped through the shelters, over the feet of dope sick dosers. Suppose the head, Elektra dreamed, could be made to fly like an airship, its eyes yellow beacons? Ilea Lark Urkl whined as Jon Hauk Or, blocked from progress, pulled apart the cladding.

"He will be crushed and we will have to fetch him back," she hissed. "He is making too much noise."

"How did they do all this?" asked the girl. "How did they take away the head?" She pulled on a pair of rubber clogs. "Where?" she asked, exasperated.

"The crowd only knows," Ilea Lark Urkl said acidly, "In its wisdom. Here, there is an ocean of idle hands. All this detritus could be sorted in a trice. But the limits of our knowledge was set by silents filming from their balconettes." The crone made to put aside her embroidery but seemingly thought better of it and now clung to it as if to wrench further meaning from her past work.

"Someone stuck the gates open," growled the crone, "This square was once well secured against invasion. There is a trick with wooden shims anyone can learn to do. Destroys rod iron in seconds. And nobody said a word. They pulled down the cavalier. Or tried to. The reached the limit of their art. Now everybody eats everybody's food. Now we mumble." She looked closely at her cloth, knotted a thread, bit at it, spit out the tag end. Elektra looked about for a coat and, finding none, drew the blanked about her shoulders. "How far," inquired the crone querulously, "do you think you can get in those shoes?"

Jon Hauk Or had passed through the barrier and bent his body to go up the thumb. Once atop he climbed it as if it were a stair. Then he walked confidently across the broad verdigris palm. The preceptor had the air about him of a person who knew he was being watched and recorded, had about him the extra vibrancy exhibited by the player for whom one was rooting. He stretched to catch at the gilded braiding. This made a ripple visible across his back when he pulled himself up. He proceeded on all fours up the bicep. There came a brief flash as he welded an anchor for his line above the cavity where the cavalier's arm had once joined the torso.

In Elektra's memory he waved. Jon Hauk Or sat with his legs apart and the sun on his face. He waved or he didn't wave. What is indelible to Elektra's memory is the preceptor's slow fall backwards from sight. Jon Hauk Or was going nowhere fast one moment, seemingly content, his eyes to the sky, his arms out as if for a morning stretch. Next, there was nobody.

"What is he looking for?" asked the girl.

"Bones, the insides of them, and whatever is beyond marrow, capsules, time," said the crone wiggling her fingers in the air, "A spark."

"I feel I should help," said Elektra, "I feel my place is outside."

"You are no simple penal," spat Ilea Lark Urkl, "And your place will not be at the glass." The girl thought the crone rose to throw her a slap and winced in anticipation. But she only patted Elektra on the shoulder. "Besides. We don't even know your real name. Abide with me a while. If you go, nobody will come looking."

They sat together waiting for Jon Hauk Or, the girl and the crone, until the girl found herself alone, another day gone by. Bored beyond imagining any future action, every corner of the nursery explored, the girl kicked off her ridiculous rubber clogs and touched the mesh for the first time.

For a moment it showed a face alive with the same tremors and tics as her own. Hair like straw, a bit too dry. Green eyes slightly askew. Natural teeth, though stainless and small, like little rows of new corn. A great youthful pressure pushing out from her brow. The ghost, however, was then marked with her father's frown. THERE IS NO ENEMY, appeared in block letters overcoming her reflection across the brow. The hues sweetened from red to blue to violet then effervesced.

Her search began with mumbles, chirps, fragments of half-formed grammar and malapropisms, a desperation of words overheard and filtered through from the companionway these last days. There was such error in her speech it cannot be laid off upon her poor dentition.

Whatever Elektra mispronounced the mesh endeavored to put it right. The girl was still so unsure of the sound she made in the world. She did not speak up even when prompted. She had never said "necessary" and transposed the *v* and *l* in "cavalier." She took a deep breath and imagined speaking to the pig she raised one season. The mesh simplified what she said to images, a selection at which she could simply paw. Eventually the machine spoke in a voice which put pressure behind every word. She waved past maps of their progress, the sites, the locations of arcades, the history of the concentration city, the composition of the chartreuse pool, an elementary exposé dealing with the gantries. Finally, she came upon the story about the statue.

Bron Ignaz, popularly known as the artist Aliunde, began the sketches upon the first rumors of the cavalier's malaise, although it was understood the ultimate commission would be in bronze. The cavalier's daughter, who keyed a somber melody in the music room looking out on the grove of their estate, had noticed him linger in his armchair past his usual hour. That night the old usurper stood to deliver a blessing but the words from his heart could not be pushed beyond his lips.

It is said Aliunde's initial work betrayed too much haste, that he relied too heavily upon stock depictions conjured from the crown archive. Which perhaps explains the blocked-in treatment of his mount. At the time Aliunde was pressing together his first wax models, the cavalier's palsies were dismissed as rumor. His then-recent public meeting of provosts of the varsity was offered as counter story and his steady invocation were entered into record without remark. Nevertheless, Aliunde's understudies suggested he travel to the cavalier's bedside by suborbital air. So much had to be set into motion before working in noble metal.

While the caisson and the forge were assembled, a former aide-de-camp visited the studio. He corrected the wax profiles from memory, explaining he had often watched the cavalier backlit against the tent flap while on campaign.

Hope was entertained the cavalier might rally but only his legend remained by morning. Far away, the spirit had gone out of his features. Later, before the dailies broadcast confirmation, certain intelligence of his demise arrived in the form of a heavy box, which contained his death mask.

Aliunde regarded it for a morning, laid out on velvet. The statuary had already progressed beyond correction. Bron Ignaz held the beloved visage in his hands and knew he had made the nose too aquiline, yet the apprentices

*poured oil into the molds to be followed later
that afternoon by the bronze.*

*As it cooled there was an argument as to
whether the cavalier had ever really accepted a lady's white plume to adorn his hat. The
aide remembered no such shadow, yet there
were images taken on raids upon then-unin-
corporated cities which showed its white shock
clearly floating among garlands thrown by the
liberated.*

Elektra's eyes filled with the orange blos-
som which bloomed over the square. The
fiery bloom stood on a shrieking tower of
smoke. Its glare persisted enough to see low
and slinking figures begin to infiltrate from
the locks of a dry canal which bordered one
side of the square. Another bloom rose and
popped, green this time. The crowd grew up
under a burning sky. The figures stood once
they had grown in sufficient number.

"They are coming to warm themselves," said
Ilea Lark Urkl. "Bone people before a false fire."

Now the skels and tribesmen were numerous enough that they dared stand less beast-
like. Present to their own company they drew
up to each other as straight as possible and
were almost proud. The joggles and mysterians,
excited by the fireworks, continued to congre-
gate but could only concentrate in the spaces
amid the wreckage. Their spheres of devotion
were too small, the sight lines of mutual regard

too broken, for the crowd to organize toward an objective. They were nothing like the tribes that Elektra had seen thronged on the mesh. They looked about the cluttered square, abandoned spectators outside a canceled show, wondering what was about to begin. The sky had burned briefly. Was that it? They were discussing whether to disperse, where to rally in that case, how to make best use of the night.

Ilea Lark Urkl chuckled. She folded her embroidery, finished. Her little claw-like hands were a long time smoothing the cloth. She looked over a long distance. "Finished," she said, "Or nearly so."

The sky shaded to red, then the color ceased abruptly as it were a swiftly passing front. Ilea Lark Urkl sucked her teeth. "Someone wanted to get up to something," she said, "Failed."

"Go away," said the girl. "I want to sleep." She had come to think of the nursery as hers. Even the banquette by the mesh now bore her scent. "Please," she insisted.

"It is our lot to sit together." Ilea Lark Urkl chuckled and patted the cot beside the girl. Elektra let her hip be drawn into the slight depression the crone's weight made in the mattress. She closed her eyes and shivered to feel the crones fingers pulling lightly at her hair. "Someone has to explain the city."

"I want to see my mother," said Elektra. The girl drew in a sharp breath as if had forgotten a critical chore, as if she had forgotten to fodder the cow. "Where is my brother?" she asked. "I've forgotten my brother."

"I have this for you instead."

Across her mottled arms now was a sable scarf woven of same material as the preceptors' robes. The girl sat up in bed, passing the scarf through her hands. "Where are the charms?" she asked, "It is innocent of the laws.

"Look again," said the crone "Black is not absence. Or filth." The woman drew the curtain and put on the lights. "Don't worry," she said, "We cannot be seen."

"It is all black," said Elektra pawing at the scarf, uncomprehending.

"Every thread across your palm is law." The crone laughed, pleased the girl had spoken according to expectation. "It is black with law. Their mass is as solid as all power. They only seem a block in poor light. Or when seen from our true vantage." The crone pointed to the ceiling. "From below."

"More light," snapped Elektra at the mesh in the tone she'd heard Ilea Lark Urkl use. Upon closer inspection, the cloth was indeed a mess of twists and backstitch. The girl could make out letters only after a moment and angling her hands held out flat. Her eye or mind was not yet equal to teasing out any precept.

"What are they? The laws? Are they long? The words of them, I mean."

"For me to find out," said the crone, rolling up her needles and hoop, "And you to know."

Elektra looked back at the crone abjectly, a young mother defied.

"That is for you to say," said the crone. "Hush. We will be moving soon."

In the dark, the girl worried her way deeper into her wrist. She pressed and scraped, seeking to stroke the warm back of the frog that made its bed just under her wrist bone. She put the scarf over her eyes, but could not sleep.

"Open the window again," said Elektra, "They bear watching."

There were no more fireworks over the square. In the close spaces and the growing dark brawls were stoked. A man beat a brat who had not been nimble enough. The boy landed on a leg already broken and fell from view.

"Savory is to your taste?" asked the controller Prather, "Forgive me, I forgot to ask."

She sat up. She folded the sheet to hide the spotting only to uncover more, then noticed her wrist now wore a bandage.

"I took the liberty," said Prather, "Later we will have new sheets."

"Are we moving?" she asked the steward.

In way of answer, the controller raised the blind. The girl watched for changes in the scene through the steam rising from her cup of Skiboo. The arm. The wrecks. Morning smokes hanging low in the air. She was not thirsty but liked the steam on her cheeks. The sky was lead scud and sent down tendrils to meet the cookfires. She could just make out the bright weld where Jon Hauk Or had attached his line. She was satisfied the disorder was no sinister than the evening before.

For a while she became occupied with the secret sentences she would tease out of the city. She resolved to find a law to bring her mother back, remedy her brother's absence. There must be a penalty for falling down a well. If it would help, she would find the ordinance which would repair the cavalier and silence the thunder of the passing articulated, calm the instinct for ambush. She would address whatever was the strongest noise deranging the land of the crowd, maybe make a speech from the back of a wagon. Maybe she would ride a horse herself. She could maybe step up to cheers with the laws wrapped warmly around her neck. Or perhaps she was to be expelled at some subsequent stop, expelled to a crooked byway, thrown to a crowd compressed to frenzy by all the doors closed against them.

"Considering tall orders over a cup of Skiboo?" asked Prather, "The best part of waking up."

"Prather," said the girl, "You let him go out alone. Why?"

Prather opened his mouth but thought better of speaking. He turned instead to greet the crone. "I can make it sweet," he said, "Sweet Skiboo all around? It would be no trouble."

"By no means," exclaimed Ilea Lark Urkl, dismissing him with a wave. "Why aren't we already moving?" she asked after Prather turned to leave with the linen towel on his shoulder.

"Shall I release a skutter?" he said apologetically, "Or don't you think so?" He excused himself, receiving no answer. "I'm sorry, I don't know how to address you."

"You say 'excellency' as you would with any other preceptor," growled Ilea Lark Urkl.

"I wasn't speaking to you, excellency," he said. "I meant your charge, the transport. The rescue."

"He hasn't been gone long enough," said the crone.

"Excellency, at this moment we are at the point of budgetary indifference. His absence makes this stop, the stag, or whatever they are calling this shambles these days, his final destination. The difference is almost exactly the expense for a skutter." Prather stood in the door. "I will move without further order on the hour."

"Release a skutter," said Elektra, "Please."

"As you have read, I cannot ask you for your name," said Ilea Lark Urkl, "The law says it must be given freely."

The girl simply blinked back. "Please," she said, "What is a skutter? I heard you speak of one before. What does it do?"

"Evacuation. Seeing hidden scenes. Small feats of larceny. When such needs arise and expenses permit, we send out a skutter." She barked into the mesh. "Yes. Release a skutter. Economy model." Ilea Lark Urkl raised her sleeves, revealing the spotted flesh the girl expected, but also an ornate wristwatch within whose large face bloomed an array of movements. She tapped it.

"We have two days," she said flatly. "There it goes now."

Elektra followed her finger to a dwarfish creature dressed in rags and a pointed cap. It picked a path across the carriageway poorly. There was something amiss with its hips or else its legs were cut to different sizes. It made Elektra think of the chicken she once dressed up to terrify her brother.

"That's it?" asked Elektra, "Is it hurt?"

"The skutter," said Ilea Lark Urkl, "Is only a type of servitor. Dear and curious. Disguised with cloth and what-have-you but hard beneath. I'll grant you it looks ragged. Its gait is a deliberate sham to make one look away." The preceptor drew her robes about her. "Now, let us take in what it sees and hears."

The skutter's conical hat was so visibly ridiculous it projected embarrassment back upon the witness. Negotiating a tumbled barricade of exhausted purchase servitors, plastic beams, and split palettes, the machine looked very like the chicken Elektra once tied into a doll's jacket, beheaded, and released in the dark after an evening of whispering her brother stories of a gnome their father was holding hostage in the shed. The skutter scrambled through the passenger compartment of a burned-out K-coupe without doors, then froze and fell over at the approach of a pair of joggled children. Lying in a bright green puddle it looked like any other discarded object in the general constellation of disorder present in the square, nothing worth picking up and flinging, too soggy with oil for kicking, and was probably toxic if thrown into a fire, just another plastic soyabif hull or wife beater balled, soiled, and discarded. The skutter, from its puddle of antiheat, was close enough to pick up the addled speech of the children.

"Ion even," said the pants-less male recently unsexed. He wore a ring through his nose to which was attached a fine chain. His partner or master, a child more mature by one well-fed season, held the other end. The latter's knotty skull bore two livid circles where there had recently been horns. "It so hard on my mental," he said, both emphatic, woeful, and confused. His head was so newly lightened. "Ion even eida," he agreed, looking at the skutter. Then the pants-less child shook his own chain. They shuffled on, both bleeding.

Elektra sat with Ilea Lark Urkl. "Why are so many of them chained together?" asked the girl, "This is at least the second time."

"In a penury of law," croaked Ilea Lark Urkl, "Chains are the first resort of those who seek security. Perhaps the only one."

They turned toward the mesh and they saw what the skutter saw. They watched joggles filter in and out of the square by pairs and bands, carrying handisaks pregnant with sloshing liquid and what appeared to be rude dirt. Through the skutter, they watched the inept installation of generators, crushed toes, family-style feedings conducted on cable trunnions, the flash and wounding scatter resulting in poor bonfires into which batteries had been thrown, the fuel having to be regathered after the inevitable explosion. Throughout, Ilea Lark Urkl remained attentive for any sign of Jon Hauk Or. "He sometimes leaves an operational signal in chalk at knee height," she explained, "Peel your eyes for a rune which looks like a heavenward fish or boat." The skutter continued its circuit of the pedestal, occasionally flitting through open spaces like a grasshopper, suddenly cheating gravity to alight on a spar. It dropped before it could be spotted and called out, breaking its fall on a shelter half, rolling down to clatter into a wide depression.

"Ah ha," said Ilea Lark Urkl with delight she did not try to conceal. Her giggle startled the girl from her doze. "See that? See the spot?" said the crone. "The depression? This is the spot where the statuary's head must have come to rest." There the skutter righted itself, bent, replaced its hat, and made its way gaily into a septic culvert where it sat out the rising activity in the square.

The crone and the girl continued to watch into the skutter's night. The joggles got themselves up into a dance which began slowly but was clearly headed toward frenzy. "You should maybe sleep again," said Ilea Lark Urkl, "Joggle rites are sometimes disturbing, always terrible."

"What do they do?" asked Elektra. The girl sat straighter, so to better see, opened her eyes wider, held by the dancers' dips and strides. She was surprised by their grace.

"Discuss the weather," said Ilea Lark Urkl. She clicked her teeth. By the way they clacked about Elektra understood they were false. "They make more joggles, girl."

So Elektra prepared. She wrapped herself tighter in the laws. A vulgar tone, half peal half clatter, a sound born of a broken bell invaded their attention. The girl and crone saw the first new figures transit into the wide square, pick their way toward the pedestal, each lingering to bong a pipe against the hollow arm as if to announce themselves, before they disappeared beyond the reach of the skutter's thermals.

As these horned and naked figures melted away, girl had the notion that they were drawing near to the articulated. She made ready for flight, her feet up off the floor, watching sideways, half shielded by her pillow. Ilea Lark Urkl turned down the mesh as the night hunters slowly peeled off and lingered on stools drawn to shadows. With unexpected agility, the skutter quit its vantage, kept to shadow, neared. The preceptor closed her eyes to the mesh, but could feel the hunters' presence, their necks swollen, goitered to their trunks making for such silhouettes that their human origin was obscure. The skutter tagged these figures a persistent red, extended its blade. A small white line of inelegant text appeared upon the mesh. AWAITING INSTRUCTIONS. CONFIRM. The girl opened her eyes, took in these red demons, closed her eyes again, feeling their soft presence on her consciousness, a pressure coming from beyond the wagon. The feeling was that of her mother looking in on her sleep from the top of the ladder, but colder.

"Sonic synchronization," said Ilea Lark Urkl impatiently, "Execute. Then continue."

When the noise woke Elektra, she did not recognize it as music. The mesh had been tuned out. A chant rose behind the regularity of the articulated's ventilation, which somehow drew the repetition closer. She found a corner, pushed herself into it. The words shot through the compartment and only settled into phase once she was fully awake. Their song was almost language, just over the horizon of grammar, a taunt as an invading fleet whose approaching sails could just be discerned. *Tales we win.* She lay and listened, but it was beyond the girl's ear and education. The effort to put sense to *Wale siwin* or *si win ta le* sunk her into despond. Have I no ears? she won-

dered. What is lacking in my heart? The chant
became a dance before a fire which arched
their backs and the dance descended into a
darker revel. *Wintaleslose.* Something along
those lines.

Elektra watched them eat from bowls at
bonfires. She watched them draw out coals
and eat of the fire itself. Nothing she saw
made sense. The noise had grown with the
number of skulkers. Their chant never wavered, the voices somehow traveling, raised.
Each hour grew darker as their fires were
consumed. At times she felt the breezes
as if she were no longer contained within
the articulated. She watched them copulat-
ing, firelit, in the scattered excelsior of rup-
tured shipping. From their mouths came a
limey froth. Once it all grew too terrible she
turned away. Her limit was reached at the
bright slash of the unsexing of a bare-chest-
ed man. He had not died as one might expect. He danced with red hands. When she
could look again she saw a woman seated,
her head daubed in clay by her attendants,
until a large hive sat upon her shoulders.
Across the mute surface a rudimentary face
was sketched out in pitch. Whatever they
had been before, packers or mysterians or
wayward silents, they were now what Jon
Hauk Or and Ilea Lark Urkl called joggles.
No god made them. They made themselves.
They came from the crowd itself, polliwogs

stirred up from a clay bank in bad water. Even the skies seemed pregnant with toxic promise.

From the porthole, they could not discern the skutter. They had spotted no operational rune. The chant now ceased. The bands broke apart and reformed just beyond the glow. They ambled about, tanglefooted, raging, yet somehow withheld. They raised and discarded spars and cobbles and put them down again, forever searching for a better implement. They came back into light, became frightened if alone, passed behind screening fascines woven of discarded strapping, disappeared into tents, rolled themselves into plastic hammocks, and did not re-emerge. There was the sound of constant, lurching activity, of barrels overturned, cascades of cans, orders and insubordination, the dull thuds of body blows.

Ilea Lark Urkl returned from whatever errand had drawn her away. The girl could feel the crone's crablike presence at her back.

"Should we recall the skutter?" asked the girl. "What are they about to do?"

"They sent their signal up too early," chuckled Ilea Lark Urkl, "See how even now they wander off at the edges?" The girl did not see this. The joggled mass was assembling to a ragged line along the carriageway. Marshals climbed the shoulders and held the horns of their mounts and looked back into the crowd, surveying its density. Yet none dared raise a blade or bar to signal a general advance across the bright white limit of the carriageway.

"What signal?" asked the girl.

"Did you notice the sky burn, dear? For the whole day. Remember?"

"That was their doing? How?"

Ilea Lark Urkl let loose a windy sigh of disgust. "Just another trick. Anybody who has gone to school can do it." The crone rubbed her eyes. "Or even if you haven't," she grumbled, impatient with herself, "Obviously."

"Why won't they go away?" the girl whined, "They're so terrible."

"They scent something sweet on the air."

"Jon Hauk Or is inside the statue."

"I suppose. Yes. But that is not what they smell." The crone pinched Elektra who pulled her arm away.

"This pack still hasn't found its nose. It is leaderless and doesn't know which way to break. And will be this way for a while."

"When they do decide?"

"Concentration. Pressure. Direction. They always get their man."

"What happens when they do?"

"The usual," said Ilea Lark Urkl, "Nothing subtle or slow. How open were your eyes? They bend him over and make him a king." The girl looked at the crone, uncomprehending.

"How much have you taken on in this past day, girl?"

"Enough," dared Elektra, "Please, do not wake me any more today."

Early next morning, socked in under cover of soft banks of a low and heavy mist came a dry rattle and crash. The line of joggles had withdrawn. Elektra released the gasket and drew up the shade. The settled mist revealed the slight slope of the square, the stag still carrying the twice-maimed cavalier as if across a snow field. Her ears popped and sharpened each time she caught the sporadic footsteps of a small pack on the move. The mist, a stew of camp smoke and cleanser and diverse excrements, slipped toward the plinth, eliding the lower rubble, concealing whatever moved beneath.

Then she saw the skutter. The girl knew it by its conical hat, which hopped up from this chemical nightmare with the speed of hopper disturbed from its stalk, arcing high into the statue's palm. There it stuck. By night it had buried its head in a pile of char and packaging. Now it moved up the cavalier's severed hand with the aid of some hidden adhesive, an agile rat on a rafter. The skutter jogged up the arm and stood before the cavity where the arm had once been joined to the statue. It opened its mouth wide and shone down a bright beam which strobed briefly. It let off a spark which rose and dove, a weighty hornet making the cavity buzz. Elektra heard a muffled boom shortly thereafter. The dregs of black vapor rose from the hole. The skutter stood on the edge and did an awkward pirouette. It lost equilibrium, discarding itself with a violent sideways leap. She listened to it banging down the bicep.

The skutter settled at the bottom, its gyroscopes failed, its hat lost. It moved crablike on its intact limbs, on a weird diagonal, half a roll, half a crawl and fell into a further hole where the elbow of the arm had pushed beyond the cobblestones.

That afternoon, when it seemed to Elektra another day would be lost waiting with the crone, John Hauk Or filled the mesh. He was crouched over in a close space, lit by the skutter's torch, the light at his face at times unsteady, ready to fail. The preceptor's voice, when he was recalling his previous life, brightened with humor but otherwise wallowed in a register as besmirched as his face. Interference of some sort choked his voice to a whisper at times, a flurry of leaves to Elektra.

"I made my way down the arm easily enough. A long amusing slide. I suppose you saw me go in from the articulated if you happened to be looking. At the bottom of the elbow there is an access way cut down from within. Where I find myself now. Connects with the sewers for a short span. The regularity of the passage is almost reassuring, nothing

like what one finds later. I suppose I'm somewhere beneath the statue unless I miscounted
my paces. The point is, I am coming to you
from somewhere deep inside and downward.

"Lately, I have been making my way back
by the traces I swiped into the glow. I apol-
ogize for my state of undress. There is a re-
sidual luminescence on the cooler surfaces by
which I make way. I have no idea of the hour.
I wonder if I have ever left the interior of the
cavalier.

"I am far from alone. Down here there
are naked crowds. I have been drinking from
pools of seepwater. I divested myself of the
laws to better fit in. To better fit in I rolled
in mire until I dulled my color to them. I go
naked as they do, carrying my shoes and my
laws in a bundle as I have seen others do.

"I believe this was within the pedestal, another tunnel winding inward, always down. It
is hard to judge. I am trying to return to where
the elbow meets the surface. Maybe the skutter will spell me out."

Jon Hauk Or drew his hand down his face
and sighed. "I pressed on for what seemed
days hoping to find the sun streaming down
from the cavalier's neck." The preceptor tilted
his head and in the skutter's eye his face became foreshortened, grotesque. "This little guy
looks like he's on his last legs."

A sharp rap jolted the image before it
cleared and brightened.

"I came to the back of a crowd just milling about, waiting to advance. The heat is heavy, biological. Advancing was not the relief I imagined it would be. There are so many more down here than you would imagine. We shuffle forward a few steps, bump to a stop. All the traffic goes one way. I boarded a boat, stepped off a metal pier into a flat-bottomed boat. There was a whole line of them. I did not see the end. Doubling back was no easy thing. I stepped out and walked back through chill waters." Jon Hauk Or's features were becoming flatter and slack, as if he were going to sleep. "Mine are not the only traces," he continued, "There are images of what I take to be bison, elk, herds of men on all fours."

"Have you found the capsule?" asked Ilea Lark Urkl sharply. This brought the man back to himself and, for a moment, his face was inhabited by its former humor. He raised his eyebrows in surprise.

"Did you find the bones?" asked Ilea Lark Urkl, speaking over the beginnings of the preceptor's answer to her first question. He coughed wetly. He held a copper-colored egg before the skutter, slightly larger than his fist. He squeezed it until there came a pop and cascade of objects fell from the skutter's view.

The preceptor searched about and held up a mirrored cut which caused the skutter's image to flare. "This was a plate portrait, I suppose. There are many of these, similarly denatured. Loved ones and enemies, by tradition. Departed now, by the magic of photodegradation. Alchemy would be the only hope."

Jon Hauk Or considered the next object closely before holding it to the skutter's eye and chuckled.

"A doubloon. Struck with the profile of the Hill Eater on both faces. Two headed. Does this bring you back the varsity, crone?"

Elektra saw she was indeed smiling, her dead teeth wide. "To teach the names of the usurpers. Their order of succession. Also used to dispense with those who chose tails," explained Ilea Lark Urkl winking at the girl, "You'll see. The Victory Game was still current in my varsity days."

"There are many texts," said Jon Hauk Or, "Children's rude scrawls. Tasteful verses unbound but set into tiny boxes. None I will belabor you the reading. Bones are general but recent and disassociated. These are not the bones we are looking for."

"But have you accounted for the head?" asked the crone, "Did you see from the inside?"

"Maybe they invented a new tool?" ventured the girl.

"By no means," snorted Ilea Lark Urkl patting her arm, "Be still and listen."

"I had never climbed," said Jon Hauk Or again growing absent and slack. "I remember I expected to see light from within. I imagined I would find some way up and examine

212

the cut. There are hands enough down here to achieve anything. Whenever I think I'm ascending my efforts are inverted by some trick of the dark. I feel the effort in my legs as expected but then find the weariness transferred to my shoulders and then find myself moving on all fours. Whatever margin remains to me will soon be exhausted. Do not defend me to Prather. I will steal no more daylight. Proceed when necessary."

The mesh was dark.

Elektra, abandoning her wrist, instead pulled a black thread. It came away easily leaving the white words SEE YOU ON THE OTHER SIDE ruled upon the hemline in small capitals.

The crone dozed in her sunbeam when the articulated hummed and abruptly rose. The day was clear. The girl watched joggles coursing some unpunished man, still afar. Through the ruin he ran as the war pack formed up behind a single horned youth in a loin cloth, joggles painted and daubed with sauces and varnish and blood, a wave of furious clowns, raising a hilarity of bent spars above their painted heads.

The crone snorted and came awake. She oriented herself by following Elektra's gaze to the scene. "Here comes more tenderness," the crone said disapprovingly.

The man was long-limbed like the scarecrow her father refreshed and put out before sowing. Somehow, wheeling and faking and springing the longest lines he could find free of obstacle, he retained his hat. The girl continued to watch, her heart caught up at once with the pack and their quarry. Surrounded though he was, he feinted his way confidently past joggles too eager to tackle. He turned sharply, removed a shoe, and threw it at a ram-horned joggle with a belly like a cauldron. This demon batted away the missile, but the distraction bought the man a breath of wind. Would he regret this bravado, wondered the girl. The man, growing distinct, veered for the carriageway.

Elektra wished the articulated would depart just then. She wanted the man to escape, just not to her. He was her brother divided in that moment, maybe, and her father, all at once. Someone pursued by furies. Elektra wanted him caught. She wanted to be spared the sight. She wanted to see what would happen. She wanted to be the one to decide.

"What will happen," asked the girl imitating the crone's dry superiority, "When these people discover teamwork?"

"Those are not people," laughed Ilea Lark Urkl. She drew closer. "You should see what they get up to with gas."

"I want to go outside," said the girl, "He needs help."

Ilea Lark Urkl was spreading a length of white linen across her lap. Motes rose in the glare. "Soon you will sing outside. Everyone will hear you. Until then, hide your light and close your mouth, Elektra."

"Shouldn't we stay?" ventured the girl.

"By no means. There is a vast concert of schedules and budgets underlying everything. Quite beyond the capacity of any one Prather or his machines. There is a great snarl of event, nodes of indifference, orbital variance. Most are pushed into event. You are for transport. It is not your turn."

"My name—" began Elektra cannily, as if to offer a substitute invented on the spot. Her secret had only echoed in her ear. She was now unsure whether the crone had truly used it.

"Your name your father gave up for nothing," said Ilea Lark Urkl, "Or weren't you listening?"

Elektra looked hard at the man, wanting to be at his side. The crowd that was now rallying to the cries. New packs were forming, wheeling about, becoming excited, waiting for direction.

"Thunda," they chanted, "thunda, thunda, thunda."

"If you go now," said the preceptor, "It is certain you will not be where you are needed."

"I'm needed?" asked the girl, "For what?"

"Don't be too certain," said Ilea Lark Urkl, "For I have no confirmation of the contrary."

They were now slowly crossing into the shadow of the mutilated colossus.

"Former men, women, and children," continued the crone, "Lions and tigers and bears given to their animal humors. One day you will question the utility of the law. The utility of the law is the law itself. You will descend and speak the law, maybe. But leave it alone for now." The crone set to her knots and needles and designs, her voice now a murmur replete with dread. "Send me a one-way bird if you ever learn the answer. What is the utility of men, and women, and children. Why can't they just let it all be?" Out there, somewhere far behind, her father was bringing a hammer down on a beast. Her brother was beside him, seeing what the plowman sees in the morning. Out there, her mother burned.

The escaping man now ran a beeline toward the slowly moving articulated.

"Deblayment?" offered Elektra. Her mouth felt full of the strength of the new word.

"This is not for me to say," said the crone, shivering in the sun. "I have no such the authority." She drew her arms to her sides, teeth chattering. "It is," she said, "For you."

Elektra put her hands to porthole, drew the world close.

Prather lost his controller's shako when he hit the flat. Without it he did not look like Prather. She had the brief impression that ordering a cup of Skiboo might summon him to her, might save him. He was trying to get out of his jacket when they caught up. So, he

216

had left his budgets open on the mesh and gone out for the preceptor, a coil of line over his shoulder. She wanted to leave this world with no statues, travel to the one just beneath, the one of usurpers, and finally the first king. Either would be more noble.

By then they had crossed into the sun again and she could make the view no larger. Prather was taken under.

"Soon I will be bald and blind," said the crone. These were among the last words Ilea Lark Urkl would speak to her charge, "See there is no statue." Even then, Elektra was shocked by the crone's delusion.

There follow more elegant vicinages, the air now densely brined by a nearby sea. Elektra abandoned the frog in her wrist. She let herself heal. She forgot her mother. She pulled a new thread from the scarf. She pulled away mysterious commandments, taking them into memory. A clash law. A physical law. Torts. A poetic line. The threads gather above her head like flying straw, dissipate when she is not looking.

On the day Elektra is received into the varsity she remembered the rused ignorance of her first preceptors. This is not the day she will spend her name by speaking it aloud to the bursar standing before the great door. She knows her name has and will go out be-

fore her. She is to be the two-faced coin to be
passed in a secret clasp by those who know
her price.

But first the test.

"Heads," she said upon the toss.

Sex,
Books,

&
SHAGDUK

a novel of 1977

jb jackson

Kickstarter March 2022 pilumpress.com

RETVRN

SCHUYLER HERNSTROM

thune's vision

This book was my only company in a lonely time. Simply xcellent!
Lone Wolf

A classic collection.
Three new fictions.
Monkeyshines.

Pilum Press Trade Edition
Kickstarter in 2022
www.pilumpress.com

Visit pilumpress.com today!